NOT FIT
FOR A KING?

NOT FIT
FOR A KING?

BY

JANE PORTER

All the characters in this book have no existence
outside the imagination of the author, and have
no relation whatsoever to anyone bearing the same
name or names. They are not even distantly inspired
by any individual known or unknown to the author,
and all the incidents are pure invention.

First published in Great Britain 2011
by Mills & Boon, an imprint of Harlequin (UK) Limited.
Large Print edition 2012
Harlequin (UK) Limited, Eton House,
18-24 Paradise Road, Richmond, Surrey TW9 1SR

© Jane Porter 2011

ISBN: 978 0 263 22569 3

Harlequin (UK) policy is to use papers that are natural,
renewable and recyclable products and made from
wood grown in sustainable forests. The logging and
manufacturing process conform to the legal environmental
regulations of the country of origin.

Printed and bound in Great Britain
by CPI Antony Rowe, Chippenham, Wiltshire

For Tessa Shapcott,
who bought my first book in January 2000
and changed my life forever!

PROLOGUE

Palm Beach, Florida

"You *do* look like me." Princess Emmeline d'Arcy's voice was hushed as she slowly circled Hannah, her arched eyebrows pulling over deep blue eyes. "Same face, same height, same age…if our hair color was the same…we could pass for twins. Incredible."

"Not exactly twins. You're half my size, Your Highness," Hannah said, suddenly self-conscious next to the very slim Princess Emmeline. "Itty-bitty, as we say in America."

Princess Emmeline didn't appear to hear her, too busy examining Hannah from head to toe. "Do you color your hair? Or is that natural? Either way, it's gorgeous—such a rich, warm shade of brown."

"It's from a box. It's several shades darker than my natural color, and I do it myself," Hannah stammered.

"Can you buy your color here in Palm Beach?"

Hannah couldn't believe that the stunning golden-blond princess would be interested in her shade of brown hair dye. "I'm sure you can—it's sold everywhere."

"I meant, could *you* buy it for me?"

Hannah hesitated. "I could. But why would you want it, Your Highness? You're stunning, so beautiful as you are."

Princess Emmeline's full lips curved and yet her expression looked bleak. "I thought maybe for a day I could be you."

"What?"

The princess walked away from Hannah, moving to stand at one of the tall windows of her lavish hotel suite where she gazed out over the hotel's elegant, tropical Florida garden.

"I've made a terrible mess of things," Princess Emmeline said softly, hands lifting to press against the glass as if she were a captive instead of the world's most celebrated young royal. "But I can't even leave here to sort things out. I'm followed wherever I go—and it's not just the paparazzi—but my bodyguards, my secretary, my ladies-in-waiting." Her slim shoulders shifted and her fingers curled until her hands were fists against the glass. "For just one day I want to be normal. Ordinary. Maybe then I could take care of something, make this nightmare I'm in go away."

The anguish in Emmeline's voice made Hannah's chest squeeze tight. "What's happened, Your Highness?"

Princess Emmeline gave her head the slightest shake. "I can't talk about it," she said, her voice breaking. "But it's bad… It'll ruin everything…"

"Ruin what, Your Highness? You can tell me. You can trust me. I'm very good at keeping secrets and would never break your confidence."

The regal princess lifted a hand to her face and swiftly wiped away tears before turning from the window to look at Hannah. "I know I can trust you. That's why I'm asking for your help."

The princess took a deep breath. "Tomorrow, switch places with me for the afternoon. Be me and stay here in the suite and I'll be you. I won't be gone long—a couple of hours, four or five at the most—and then I'll return and we'll switch back again."

Hannah sat down in the chair next to her. "I want to help you, but I have to work tomorrow. Sheikh Al-Koury doesn't give time off, and even if he did, I don't know the first thing about being a princess."

Emmeline crossed the rich crimson carpet to take a seat opposite Hannah's. "Sheikh Al-Koury can't make you work if you're ill. Not even he would drag a sick woman from her bed. And you wouldn't have to leave the hotel. I could book some spa treatments for you tomorrow and you could be pampered all afternoon—"

"But I sound like an American, not a Brabant royal!"

"I heard you introduce your sheikh boss in French yesterday at the polo tournament. You speak French perfectly, without even an accent."

"That's because I lived with a family in France one year during high school."

"So speak French tomorrow. It always throws Americans." Emmeline suddenly grinned. "We can do this. Bring hair color with you in the morning, a blond color for you and your chestnut color for me, and we'll do our hair and change clothes and think what an adventure it'll be!"

There was something infectious in Princess Emmeline's laugh and Hannah reluctantly smiled back. If Hannah had met the princess in school she would have wanted to be her friend. There was something special about Emmeline, something engaging. "It'd only be for a couple of hours, just tomorrow afternoon. Right?"

Emmeline nodded. "I'll be back before dinner."

Hannah chewed the inside of her lip. "Will you be safe, going out on your own?"

"Why wouldn't I? People will think I'm you."

"But you're not doing anything dangerous, are you? Putting yourself in harm's way?"

"Absolutely not. I'm staying in Palm Beach, not traveling anywhere. Say you'll help me, Hannah, please."

How could Hannah say no? The princess was positively desperate and Hannah had never been able to say no to someone in need of help. "I'll do it, but just for the afternoon."

"Thank you! *Merci!*" Emmeline reached out and clasped Hannah's hand in her own. "You are an angel, and you won't regret this, Hannah. I promise you."

CHAPTER ONE

Three days later—Raguva

BUT Hannah did regret it. She regretted it more than she'd ever regretted anything.

Three days had passed since she'd switched places with Emmeline. Three endless days of pretending to be someone she wasn't. Three days of living a lie.

Hannah should have stopped this yesterday before heading to the airport.

She should have confessed the truth when she could have.

Instead she'd boarded the royal jet and flown to Raguva as if she really was Europe's most celebrated princess instead of an American secretary who just happened to look like the stunning Princess Emmeline...

Should have, could have, would have...

Hannah held her breath, trying to contain her panic. She was in serious trouble now, and the only way she—and Emmeline—would survive this disaster intact was by keeping a cool head.

Not that remaining cool and calm would be easy given that she was just about to meet Princess Emmeline's fiancé, the powerful King Zale Ilia Patek, a man rumored to be as brilliant as he was driven, in front of his entire court.

Hannah knew nothing about being royal, or European. Yet here she was, squeezed into a thirty-thousand-dollar couture gown with a delicate diamond tiara pinned to her artificially lightened hair after having spent a long, and very frantic night cramming everything she could learn about Zale Patek of Raguva into her head.

Only a fool would appear before a king and his court, pretending to be his fiancée.

Only a fool, she repeated, knowing no one was holding a gun to her head, no one was forcing her to pretend to be Emmeline. No one but herself. But she'd pledged her help to Emmeline, given the princess her word. How could she abandon the princess now?

Hannah stiffened and gulped air as the tall gold and cream doors swung open, revealing the palace's grand crimson throne room.

A long row of enormous chandeliers shone so

brightly overhead that she blinked, overwhelmed by the glittering and hum of sound.

Hannah blinked again and focused on the throne dais at the far end of the room. A long red carpet stretched before her. Then a voice announced her, first in French, and then Raguvian, silencing the buzz of conversation— "Her Royal Highness, Princess Emmeline of Brabant, Duchess of Vincotte, Countess d'Arcy."

The formal introduction made Hannah's head swim. How could she have thought swapping places with Emmeline was a good idea?

Why hadn't she perceived the dangers? Why hadn't she realized that Emmeline's plan had been far from foolproof?

Because she'd been too busy enjoying the decadent spa treatments, thinking herself lucky to have this escape before she returned to her exhausting, but fascinating life as secretary for impossible to please Sheikh Makin Al-Koury of oil-rich Kadar.

Only Emmeline had never returned.

Instead she'd called and texted, begging Hannah to keep up the charade a few more hours, and then a day after that, saying there was a snag, and then another, but not to worry, everything was fine, and everything would be fine. All Hannah had to do was keep up the charade a little longer.

One of the ladies-in-waiting at Hannah's elbow whispered, "Your Royal Highness, everyone waits."

Hannah's gaze jerked back to the throne at the end of the long red carpet. It seemed so far away, but then suddenly, somehow, Hannah was moving down the plush crimson carpet, placing one trembling foot in front of the other. She wobbled in her foolishly high heels, and felt the weight of her heavy silk gown with the thousands of crystals, but nothing felt as uncomfortable as the intense gaze of King Zale Patek as he watched her from his throne, his unwavering gaze resting on her face.

No man had ever looked at her so intently and her skin prickled, heat washing through her, cheeks on fire.

Even seated, King Patek appeared imposing. He was tall, broad-shouldered and lean, and his features were handsome and strong. But it was his expression that made her breathless. In his eyes she saw possession. Ownership. They weren't to be married for ten days but in his eyes she was already his.

Hannah's mouth dried. Her heart raced. She should have never agreed to play princess here. Zale Patek of Raguva would not like being played the fool.

Reaching the dais, she gathered her heavy

teal and blue skirts in one hand and sank into a deep, graceful curtsy. Thank God she'd practiced this morning with one of her attendants. "Your Majesty," she said in Raguvian, having practiced that, too.

"Welcome to Raguva, Your Royal Highness," he answered in flawless English. His voice was so deep it whispered through her, smooth, seductive.

She lifted her head to look up at him. His gaze met hers and held, demanding her full attention. She sucked in a quick breath of surprise. This was the thirty-five-year-old king of Raguva, a country adjacent to Greece and Turkey on the Adriatic Sea. He looked younger than thirty-five. Furthermore, he was ridiculously good-looking. The photographs on the Internet hadn't done him justice.

Impressions continued to hit her one after the other—short dark hair, light brown eyes and a slash of high cheekbone above a very firm chin.

The intelligence in his clear steady gaze made her think of all the great kings and Roman rulers who'd come before—Charlemagne, Constantine, Caesar—and her pulse quickened.

He was tall, imposing, powerfully built. His formal jacket couldn't hide the width of his shoulders, nor the depth of his muscular chest. He'd been born a prince but had trained as an athlete and become a star footballer through dedication to his sport. But he'd walked away from his incredible success when his father and mother had died in a tragic seaplane accident five years ago that had taken the lives of all onboard.

She'd read that Zale Patek had rarely dated during the decade he played for two top European football clubs because football had been his passion and once he'd inherited the throne, he'd applied the same discipline and passion to his reign.

And this man, this fiercely driven man, was to be sparkling, enchanting Princess Emmeline's husband.

At the moment Hannah didn't know whether to envy her or pity her.

"Thank you, Your Majesty," she answered, slowly lifting her head to look into his eyes. His gaze met hers squarely and she felt a sharp jolt to her heart, her chest squeezing tight in protest.

It was like a thunderbolt of sensation—hot, electric—and her knees buckled, and her whole body felt weak.

Trembling in her heels, she watched King Patek rise and descend the steps of the dais. He reached for her hand, carried it to his mouth, brushing his lips across the back of her knuckles. The touch of his mouth sent yet another shudder through her, her body tingling from head to toe.

For a moment silence hung over them, surrounded them, an intimate, expectant silence that made her grow warm and her cheeks burn. Then King Patek turned her around to face his court. Applause filled the Throne Room and before she knew it, King Patek was introducing her to the first of his many advisors.

Moving down the crimson carpet, the king would pause to introduce her to this important person or that, but the sensation of his skin against hers made it impossible for her to concentrate on anything. The names and faces blurred together, making her head swim.

Zale Patek was in the middle of introducing Emmeline to yet another member of his court, when he felt her hand tremble in his. Glancing down at her, he saw fatigue in her eyes and a hint of strain at her mouth. Time for a break, he thought, deciding the rest of the introductions could wait until dinner.

Exiting the Throne Room, Zale led her through a sparsely furnished antechamber, and then a small reception room, ending in the Silver Room, a room that had been a favorite of his mother's.

"Please," he said, escorting her to a petite Louis IV chair covered in a shimmering silver Venetian embroidered fabric. An oversize silver and crystal chandelier hung from the middle of the room and Venetian mirrors lined the oyster-hued silk that upholstered the walls.

It was a pretty room and it sparkled from all the silk, silver and glass, but nothing in the room could compare to the princess herself.

She was stunning.

Beyond stunning.

As well as cunning, manipulative and deceitful, which he hadn't learned until after their engagement.

It'd been a year since he last saw Emmeline—at the announcement of their betrothal in the Palace of Brabant—and they'd only spoken twice before that, although of course he'd seen her at various different royal functions while growing up.

"You look lovely," he said as Emmeline sank gracefully into the fragile chair, her full teal and aqua skirts clouding around her, making him think of a mermaid perched on a rock. And like the sirens of lore, she used her beauty to lure men in—before dashing them on the rocks.

Which wasn't a quality Zale wanted in his wife, or Raguva's future queen.

Strong, calm, steady, principled—those were the qualities he wanted, qualities he'd come to realize she didn't possess.

"Thank you," she answered, a delicate pink appearing in her flawless, porcelain skin.

The bloom of pink in her cheeks stole his breath and made his body harden.

Had she truly just blushed? Did she think she could convince him she was a virginal maiden instead of a jaded, promiscuous princess?

And yet despite all her character flaws, in person she was nothing short of physical perfection with her exquisite bone structure, cream complexion and darkly fringed blue eyes. Even as a young girl Emmeline had been more than pretty with her wide blue eyes that seemed to see everything and know far too much, but she'd grown into an extraordinary beauty.

His father had been the one to suggest Princess Emmeline d'Arcy as a suitable bride. Zale had been fifteen at the time, Emmeline just five, and Zale had been horrified by his father's preliminary arrangements. A chubby little girl with blue eyes and dimples for a future wife? But his father had assured him that she'd be a stunning woman one day, and his father had been right. There wasn't a more beautiful or eligible princess in Europe.

"You're here at last," he said, hating that he derived so much pleasure from just looking at her. He should be distant, disgusted, turned off. Instead he was curious. As well as very physically attracted.

Her head dipped. "I am, indeed, Your Majesty."

She did that so prettily, he thought, the edge of his mouth curving in a slightly cynical smile. The blushes, the shyness, the wide-eyed innocence. "Zale," he corrected. "We've been engaged this past year."

"And yet we've never once seen each other," she answered, lifting her chin, porcelain cheeks stained pink.

He raised an eyebrow. "By your choice, Emmeline, not mine."

Her lips parted as if to protest before she pressed them together again. "Did that bother you?" she asked after a moment.

He shrugged, knowing what he couldn't—wouldn't—say. That he knew Emmeline had spent the past year continuing to see her Argentine playboy boyfriend, Alejandro, despite being betrothed to Zale.

He wouldn't say that he knew her seven-day trip to Palm Beach this past week had been to watch Alejandro play in a polo match. Or that for the past several days Zale hadn't even been sure

Emmeline would actually get on the plane and come to Raguva for their wedding scheduled for June 4, ten days from now.

But she had.

She was here.

And he fully intended to use these next ten days before their wedding to discover if she was ready to honor her commitments to him, their countries and their families, or if she planned to continue playing games and playing him. "I'm glad you're here now," he responded. "It's time we began to get to know each other."

She smiled, a slow, radiant smile that lit her eyes from the inside out and he felt heat and pressure build in his chest.

How absurd that Emmeline's beauty literally took his breath away. Ridiculous that he could be so moved by a woman in a ball gown and jewels. Diamond and sapphire rings covered her fingers and the diamonds in the tiara perched on her golden head glinted, throwing off tiny prisms of light.

"So am I," she answered. "And it's a completely different world than Palm Beach."

"It is at that," he agreed, intrigued despite himself. Charmed by everything about her right now. "I'm sorry I couldn't welcome you last night when you arrived. There is so much tradition attached to the job. Five hundred years of protocol."

"I understand."

She should. She'd agreed to this arranged marriage, too, despite being passionately in love with her boyfriend of five years. "Do you need any refreshment? Dinner is at least an hour away."

"No, thank you, I can wait."

"I heard you hadn't eaten anything today, or even last night after you arrived."

She gave him a slightly mocking look, her finely arched eyebrows rising. "Which of my attendants tattled on me?"

"My cooks were worried when you refused your meals. They feared they'd failed to whet your appetite."

"Not at all. The breakfast and lunch trays looked delicious but I was very aware that at five I'd have to fit into this gown," she said with a gesture to her curvaceous body swathed in teal silk and intricate jeweled designs.

"You're not on a starvation diet, are you?"

She glanced down at her figure. "Do I look in danger of fading away?"

Zale's lips twitched. No, she did not look like she was starving. The gown's fitted bodice revealed full, firm breasts while her waist nipped in before curving out again over very feminine hips. The gown's rich hues highlighted her smooth, creamy skin, the startling blue of her eyes and the pink pout of her generous lips. She looked lush, ripe, edible.

He felt a hot shaft of desire, and Zale fought a sudden urge to touch her. Taste her. To take his tongue to her softly parted lips, to sink his teeth into their softness, then brush his lips along her satin skin—

He broke off as his body hardened, tightening, making the fit of his trousers almost unbearable. It'd been a year since he taken a woman into his bed, wanting to respect his engagement to Emmeline, but it'd been a long year and he looked forward to consummating their marriage in ten days.

Should they marry.

He glanced down at her and discovered she was staring steadily back at him, her blue gaze unflinchingly direct. As his gaze locked with hers, he felt raw, primal desire surge through him.

He'd have her, too, he vowed, even if he didn't make her his queen.

Breathlessly Hannah dropped her gaze, breaking that strange hold Zale had had on her. When looking into his eyes—all amber color and fire—she'd felt absolutely lost, snared by her senses, drowning in sex and sin.

It'd been forever since she'd felt this way.

Wanting something so much it almost hurt…

She drew a slow breath, trying to slow the racing of her heart, trying to pretend her cheeks and lips didn't burn. But oh, they did…

He was stirring something inside of her, something that hadn't been stirred in years…

It'd been a long, long time since she'd been serious about anyone, and even longer since she'd wanted to be loved by anyone. Hannah enjoyed sex when shared with someone special. The trouble was, there hadn't been anyone special, not since she graduated from Texas A&M University four years ago. Twenty-one and thrilled to have earned her degree, Hannah had expected her college boyfriend to propose. Instead he broke up with her, announcing that he was ready to move on and begin seeing other women.

But now, for the first time since Brad had dumped her, she felt something…

For the first time in four years she wanted something…

Restless, aching, Hannah crossed her legs beneath her gown's full silk skirt and petticoat, feeling the rasp of the lace garter belt against her thighs even as her inner thighs brushed delicate skin exquisitely bare. Emmeline's lingerie, she thought despairingly, remembering in a painful rush that gorgeous, virile Zale Patek belonged to Emmeline, too.

Hannah froze, her breath catching in her throat, shocked that she could forget for even a moment who she was, what she was doing here and why.

You are not Emmeline, she told herself furiously. *You will never be Emmeline, either.*

She rose, briefly glanced at Zale as she smoothed her skirt with quick, flustered hands. "If there's time, I'd like to freshen up in my room before dinner."

"They won't even call us to the dining room for another half hour."

"Will you excuse me then?"

"Of course. I'll send someone to escort you to the dining hall when it's time."

She left the Silver Room quickly, the heavy embroidered skirts swishing as she hurried to the stairs that would take her to her suite of rooms on the second floor. Madness, madness, madness, she chanted over and over, her stomach churning, heart racing as she climbed the stairs as fast as she could.

Please let Emmeline be on the way. Please, please let there be a message from Emmeline saying she was on the plane and everything was fine and Hannah would soon be free to leave.

Inside her suite, Hannah shut the door and dashed for the nightstand next to her bed where she retrieved her phone and checked for messages, first text, then voice, but there was nothing. Nothing. Not a word.

Nothing. *Nothing!*

Hannah put a hand to her queasy middle, dangerously close to throwing up all over the green, cream and pink antique Aubusson rug beneath her feet.

It'd been hours since Emmeline's last text. Where was she? Why wouldn't she respond?

Hannah struggled to calm herself. Maybe the princess was already en route. Maybe she was on a plane flying to Raguva right now.

Hannah felt a ray of hope. It was possible. Emmeline might have been in such a hurry getting to the airport that she'd forgotten to send a message to Hannah saying she was on the way...

But even as Hannah comforted herself with the thought, the phone rang.

Emmeline.

Hannah answered immediately. "Are you here?" she asked hopefully. "Have you arrived?"

"No, I'm still in Florida," Emmeline's clipped

precise voice suddenly wobbled, sounding very far away at the other end of the line. "I'm having a bit of trouble getting out as you have my plane. Could you send it back for me?"

"Were you able to work things out?"

"N-no." Again that wobble.

"Are you okay?"

"I'm not in physical danger, if that's what you're asking."

Hannah heard the threat of tears in the princess's voice. "Things aren't going well there?"

"No." Emmeline drew a slow breath. "How is Zale? As cold as ever?"

Hannah flushed. "I wouldn't call him cold…"

"Maybe not. But he is rather grim, isn't he? I don't think he likes me much."

"He's marrying you."

"For five million Euros!"

"What?"

"Hannah, it's an arranged marriage. What did you expect?"

Hannah pictured Zale's strong, handsome face, those fiercely intelligent eyes and his tall, powerful frame. He was gorgeous. How could Emmeline feel nothing for him? "Maybe you will fall in love, once you spend time together."

"Oh, I hope not. It'd just complicate everything—" Emmeline broke off, spoke to someone in the room with her, then returned to the phone. "Good news. I don't need to wait for my plane. A friend here has a jet I can take tonight. I'll be there in the morning. Once I land, I'll text you. With any luck, no one will be the wiser."

With any luck, Hannah silently echoed, closing her phone, heart strangely heavy.

CHAPTER TWO

HANNAH told herself she was relieved that this impossible charade was nearly over. She told herself she was glad to be going in the morning. But part of her was disappointed. Zale fascinated her.

In her dressing room, Hannah touched up her makeup and adjusted the tiara before following her lady-in-waiting through soaring galleries and elegant chambers on the way to the Grand Dining Hall.

They walked briskly, her skirts whispering with every step. Passing through the Empire Room, Hannah caught a glimpse of herself in a tall mirror over the high white marble fireplace.

The reflection startled her. Is that how she really looked? Elegant? Shimmering? *Pretty?*

She shook her head at her reflection and her reflection shook her head back—pink cheeks. Deep blue eyes. High cheekbones above a generous mouth.

Hannah couldn't believe she really looked like

that. Didn't know she could look like that. She'd never felt beautiful in her life. Smart, yes. Hardworking, of course. But her father had never placed any value on physical beauty—had certainly never encouraged her to wear makeup or dress up—and for a moment she wanted to really be the beautiful girl in the mirror.

What if she was a princess in real life?

Would it change everything? Would it change her?

The lady-in-waiting paused outside tall paneled doors that opened onto the Grand Dining Hall. "We'll wait for His Majesty here," she said.

Hannah nodded, eager to see King Zale Patek again. She shouldn't care. Shouldn't feel anything.

Suddenly King Patek and his attendants were there and the atmosphere felt positively electric.

Hannah's breath caught in her throat as heat and energy crackled around them. Tall, lithe, strong, Zale Patek practically hummed with life.

She'd never met a man so vitally alive. Had never met a man with such confidence. Lifting her head she looked up into his eyes and the expression in the rich amber depths made her heart turn over.

"You look lovely," he said.

She inclined her head. "And you do, too, Your Majesty."

"I look *lovely?*"

"Handsome," she corrected, with a blush. "And royal."

He lifted an eyebrow but Hannah was saved from further conversation as the doors to the Grand Dining Hall opened simultaneously, revealing an immense, richly paneled hall easily two stories tall.

"Oh," Hannah whispered, awed by the medieval grandeur of the room. The huge room was lit almost exclusively by candlelight. Ivory tapers flickered in sconces and tall silver candelabras marched down the length of the table. Stone fireplaces marked both ends of the room and magnificent burgundy tapestries covered the richly paneled walls. The high ceiling was an intricate design of gold stencil against dark stained wood.

Zale looked down at her, a hint of a smile at his lips. "Shall we?" he asked, offering her his arm.

She looked up at him and her heart did a funny little hiccup. Beautiful face, beautiful eyes, broad shoulders, narrow waist, long muscular legs. A fantasy come to life.

Would it be such a bad thing if she were to enjoy playing Princess Emmeline for just one night?

Would it ruin everything if she liked Zale a little? Tomorrow morning she'd be heading home and would never see him again, so why couldn't she just be happy tonight?

Together they entered the crowded hall where the guests were already seated at the longest dining table she'd ever seen.

She could feel all their eyes on them, and conversation died as they walked to the two places still empty in the middle of the table. "Such a big table," she murmured.

"It is," he agreed. "Originally it was built to accommodate one hundred. But five hundred years ago people must have been considerably smaller— or perhaps they didn't mind a very tight squeeze," he answered with a hint of laughter in his voice, "because I don't think we ever seat more than eighty today."

A uniformed butler drew out a chair for Hannah while another held out Zale's and then they were sitting, and Zale leaned toward Hannah to whisper. "And even then," he added, "as you can see, eighty is still quite snug."

Snug was an understatement, she thought an hour later, feeling excessively warm and more than a little claustrophobic as the five-course meal slowly progressed. Her teal gown was too tight and pinched around her ribs, and Zale was a big man with very broad shoulders and he took up considerable space.

And then there were her emotions, which were all over the place.

Everything about him intrigued her, and it was impossible to ignore him, even if she wanted to. At least six foot three, he dominated the table with his broad shoulders and long legs.

All evening she was aware of him, feeling his warmth and energy even without touching him.

And then when they *did* touch—a bump of shoulder, a tap on the wrist and that one time his thigh brushed her own—her head spun from the rush of sensation.

Working for Sheikh Al-Koury, Hannah had arranged numerous events and dinners, and had sat next to countless wealthy men, and yet no one had ever made her feel like this before.

Nervous. Eager. Self-conscious. *Sensitive.*

Next to Zale she could hear her heart thud, feel the warmth of her breath as she exhaled, tingle with goose bumps as he turned his head to look into her eyes.

She loved that he did that. Loved that he was strong enough, confident enough, to look at a woman and hold her gaze. It was probably the sexiest thing she'd ever experienced.

But even when he wasn't looking at her, she liked the way he watched others, studying the world intently, listening with all of him—heart and mind, ears and eyes.

As one of the staff leaned over to take her plate, Hannah startled and bumped Zale.

He glanced at her with a half smile, and that barely there smile captivated her as much as his whiskey-colored gaze.

This man would be a force to reckon with—so alive, so vital—and she envied Emmeline, she did.

Imagine being loved by a man like King Patek. And that was the appeal, wasn't it? Zale wasn't a boy. He was a man. And unlike Brad, her college love, Zale was mature, successful, experienced. He was a thirty-five-year-old man in his prime.

To be loved by a man who knew what he wanted…

To be loved by a man who knew he wanted her…

Her chest squeezed hard, tight and she dragged a hand to her lap, fingertips trailing across the exquisite beading of her gown as she tried to think of something else. Something besides Zale and what was quickly becoming an impossible infatuation.

Zale's gaze met hers and held. The air bottled in her lungs. Her heart thudded in her ears.

"Not every dinner will be as long as this," he

said to her in English, his voice pitched low. They'd been switching back and forth between French and English all night for the benefit of their guests but whenever he spoke to Hannah it was in English. "This is unusually drawn out."

"I don't mind," she said, careful to speak without a hint of her Texas twang. "It's a beautiful room and I have excellent company."

"You've become so very charming."

"Haven't I always been?"

"No." His lips curved in a self-mocking smile. "You didn't enjoy my company a year ago. It was our engagement party and yet you avoided me all night." His smile didn't touch his eyes. "Your father said you were shy. I knew better."

This was a strange conversation to have here, now, with eighty people around them. "And what did you know?"

He looked at her intently, his narrowed gaze traveling slowly over her face until it rested on her mouth. "I knew you were in love with another man and marrying me out of duty."

Definitely not a conversation to be having at a formal dinner party. Nervous, Hannah rubbed her fingers against the delicate beading on her skirt. "Perhaps we should discuss this later...?"

"Why?"

"Aren't you afraid someone will overhear us?"

His gaze pierced her. "I'm more afraid of not getting straight answers."

She shrugged. "Then ask your questions. This is your home. Your party. Your guests."

"And you're my fiancée."

Her chin lifted a fraction. "Yes, I am."

He studied her for an endless moment. "Who are you, Emmeline?"

"Excuse me?"

"You're so different now. Makes me wonder if you're even the same woman."

"What a strange thing to say."

"But you are different. You look me in the eye now. You have opinions. *Attitude*. I almost think I could get an honest answer out of you now."

"Try me."

His eyes narrowed, strong jaw growing thicker. "That's exactly what I mean. You would have never spoken to me like this a year ago."

"We're to be married in ten days. Shouldn't I be forthright?"

"Yes." He hesitated a moment, still studying her. "Romantic love is important to you, isn't it?"

"Of course. Isn't it important to you?"

"There are other things more important to me.

Family. Loyalty. Integrity." He looked into her eyes then, as if daring her to disagree. "Fidelity."

Her brows pulled. "But doesn't romantic love incorporate all of the above? How can one truly love another and not give all of one's heart, mind, body and soul?"

"If you loved a man, you'd never betray him?"

"Never."

"So you don't condone affairs…no matter how discreet?"

"Absolutely not."

"You don't hope to take a lover later, after we're married and you've fulfilled your duty?"

Hannah was appalled by his questions. "Is that the sort of woman you think I am?"

"I think you're a woman who has been pressured into a marriage she doesn't want."

Her jaw dropped slightly, and she stared at him unable to think of a single response.

Zale leaned closer, his deep voice dropping even lower, his amber gaze intense. "I think you want to please others, even if it comes at a terrible price."

"Because I've agreed to an arranged marriage?"

"Because you've agreed to *this* marriage." His eyes held hers. "Can you do this, Emmeline, and be happy? Can you make this marriage work?"

"Can you?" she flashed, flustered.

"Yes."

"How can you be so sure?"

"I have discipline. And I'm older by ten years. I have more life experience and know what I need, and what I want."

"And what is that?"

"I want prosperity for my country, peace in my home and heirs to ensure succession."

"That's it? Peace, prosperity and children?"

"I'm a realist. I know I can't expect too much from life so I keep my desires simple. My goals attainable."

"Hard to believe that. You were the star foot-baller that carried Raguva to the finals of the World Cup. You don't achieve success like that without big dreams—"

"That was before my parents' death. Now my country and family come first. My responsibilities to Raguva outweigh everything else."

The fierce note in his voice made her tremble inwardly. He was intense. So very physical. Everything about him screamed male—the curve of his lip, the lean cheek, the strong masculine jaw.

"I need the same commitment from you," he added. "If we marry there will be no divorce. No room for second thoughts. No means to later opt out. If we marry it's forever, and if you can't promise me forever, then you shouldn't be here."

Zale abruptly pushed back his chair and extended a hand to her. "But that's enough serious talk for one evening. We're supposed to be celebrating your arrival and the good things to come. Let's mingle with our guests, and try to enjoy the evening."

The rest of the night passed quickly with everyone vying for an opportunity to speak with King Zale and the glamorous, popular Princess Emmeline.

But finally by ten-thirty, with the last guests departing, Zale escorted Emmeline back to her suite on the second floor.

It had been a strange evening. Perplexing, he thought, glancing down at her golden head with the delicate diamond tiara.

He'd been ambivalent about her arrival. He'd needed her here for duty's sake. Raguva needed a queen and he needed heirs. But at a purely personal level, he knew she wasn't the woman he would have ever picked as his wife.

Zale knew his faults—hardworking, no-nonsense, intensely dedicated—but he was loyal. It was a trait he respected in himself, and valued highly in others.

He realized belatedly that Emmeline might not.

He knew she'd never been spoiled by her parents. If anything, her parents had been hard on her, holding her to an exacting standard that she could never meet, which made Emmeline desperate to please. The world might see her as a glowing, confident princess but her father had warned Zale that she could be difficult and at times, terribly insecure.

King William d'Arcy's warning had worried Zale as he did not need a difficult and insecure wife, much less a fragile, demanding queen.

But Zale's late father had wanted this match very much. In his eyes, Princess Emmeline had been the perfect choice for Zale, and although his father had died five years ago, Zale wanted to honor his father's wishes, hoping that once the beautiful Emmeline reached Raguva she would settle in, settle down and become the ideal bride his father imagined her to be.

They'd reached her suite and for a moment neither said anything. "It's been a long day," he said at length, breaking the uncomfortable silence, even as he wondered how he could marry her with so many doubts.

But she was here, another part of his brain argued. She'd come when she'd said she would, and she'd behaved perfectly proper tonight. More than proper, she'd been beautiful, approachable, likable.

"It has," she agreed.

"Tomorrow night will be far less formal. There is no state dinner, just a quiet dinner together, so that should be relatively easy."

She nodded, looking up at him, her blue eyes dark with an emotion he couldn't decipher. "I'm sure it will be."

He stared down into her face, wondering how this warm, appealing woman could be the remote, cold Emmeline of the past year.

"Is there anything you need?" he asked now. "Anything that hasn't been provided?"

"Everything has been wonderful."

Her answer baffled him even more. "No special requests? You've my ear now. I'm happy to oblige."

She shook her head.

"You're happy to be here then?"

Her full mouth curved into a tremulous smile. "Of course."

He didn't know if it was the inexplicable shimmer of tears in her eyes, or that uncertain smile, but suddenly Europe's most beautiful princess looked so very alone and vulnerable that Zale reached for her, putting his hand low on her back and finding bare skin.

Her head tipped back, her blue gaze finding his. Zale's hand slipped lower, his palm sliding down warm satin skin.

He heard her soft intake of breath as he drew her closer, holding her against him, her full, soft breasts crushed to his chest. He dropped his head, covering her mouth with his.

It was to have been a brief kiss, a good-night kiss, but when her lips trembled beneath his he felt a rush of hunger. Desire.

Power.

He drew her closer still, molding her to him with pressure in the small of her back.

She shivered against him and his pulse quickened, blood pounding in his veins, making his body hot, and hard.

The need to possess her filled him, consuming him, and ruthlessly he deepened the kiss, taking her as if she already belonged to him.

The insistent pressure of his lips parted hers, and the tip of his tongue flicked the softness of her inner lip making her squirm. The urgent press of her hips against his made blood roar in his ears and he nipped at her mouth, small bites that made her shudder with pleasure.

God, she was sensitive. Responsive. Her body trembled against him, and he slid his hand from the small of her spine down, lower, over the pert curve of her backside, which made her gasp, her nipples hardening, pebbling against his chest through the thin silk of her gown.

Blood coursed through him.

Desire pounded through his veins.

She was deliciously smooth, deliciously curved and he wanted more of her, all of her. His body throbbed.

God, she was hot and tasted sweet. He wanted to rip her gown off her, strip her voluptuous body bare and explore her curves and hollows—like the dip of her spine, the space behind her knee, the softness between her thighs.

He wanted between her thighs. Wanted to part her knees as wide as he could—

Reality returned. What the hell was he doing? They were in the hall. In full view of the hidden cameras broadcasting images to his security detail.

His hand stilled on her hip. He removed the other from beneath her breast.

Slowly he lifted his head to look into her eyes. They were dark and cloudy, her lips swollen, her expression dazed.

"I'm afraid we've given my security a show," he said, voice pitched low and rough.

Color rushed into her cheeks. "I'm sorry."

He brushed a blond tendril from her flushed cheek, finding her nearly irresistible. "I'm not. Good night, Your Highness."

She looked at him for an endless moment. "Good-bye." Then she slipped into her room and closed the door.

CHAPTER THREE

ENTERING her suite Hannah gently closed and locked the door, heart racing, body shaking.

For a long moment she leaned against the locked door, a hand pressed to her mouth.

She'd kissed him. Kissed him madly, passionately, kissed him as if she were drowning, dying, and maybe she was.

How could she go tomorrow? How could she leave and never see him again?

But there was no way she could stay. He didn't want her, Hannah, he wanted Emmeline.

And even that hurt. How could he want Emmeline when the princess didn't care for him, would never care, while Hannah already cared too much…?

That was the part that confused her, infuriated her, most. How could she care already? She'd only met Zale today. She'd spent what—five hours with him? Six? Barely enough time to be infatuated. So why did she feel sick? Panicked?

Desperate?

Why did she think when she left here she'd never forget him?

Hannah choked back a frustrated cry and pressed her hand harder to her mouth to stifle the sound.

Her eyes burned and her throat ached and she hated herself for wanting something—someone— she couldn't have.

She wasn't the type of woman to set herself up for failure.

"Your Highness," Celine, Hannah's maid, said breathlessly, emerging from the dressing room, with Hannah's nightgown and robe. "I didn't hear you return. Have I kept you waiting?"

Hannah blinked back tears and pushed away from the door. "I just returned," she said, mustering a watery smile. "But I'd love your help getting out of this gown."

Leaving Emmeline, Zale forced himself to put her from his mind and focus now on other things—like Tinny.

He headed toward his own wing of the palace but first stopped at his younger brother's room. He never went to bed without a last check on Tinny.

Opening the door to Tinny's sitting room he saw that all the lights were out except for the small lamp on the top of the bookshelf on the far wall.

Tinny's night-light. He couldn't sleep without it.

Zale felt a rush of affection for his twenty-eight-year-old special-needs brother, a brother who'd needed him even more after their parents' death.

Constantine—or Tinny, as he'd always been called within the family—was to have been on the plane with his parents on that ill-fated flight, but at the last minute he'd begged his parents to let him fly to St. Philippe, their private Caribbean island, with Zale the next day instead.

Even five years later, Zale gave daily thanks that Tinny hadn't been onboard. Tinny was everything to him, and all the family he had left, but Tinny still missed his parents dreadfully, still asked for them, hoping that maybe today his beloved mama and papa would come home.

"Your Majesty," a voice whispered from the dark, and Mrs. Sivka, Tinny's evening nurse, emerged from the shadows in a dressing gown. "He's doing well. Sleeping like a lamb."

"I'm sorry I didn't come to say good-night earlier."

"He knew you wouldn't be coming. When you were here at tea this afternoon you told him tonight was a very important night." Mrs. Sivka smiled. "How did it go, Your Majesty? Is she as beautiful as they say?"

Zale felt a strange tightness in his chest. "Yes."

"Tinny can't wait to meet her. It's all he talked about today."

"He shall meet her as soon as possible."

"Tomorrow?"

Zale pictured Emmeline and then his brother, and knew that innocent, idealistic Tinny would immediately place her on a pedestal. He'd adore her, worship her and give her the power to break his heart. "Not tomorrow, but soon, I promise."

"He'll be disappointed it's not tomorrow."

"I know, but there are a few wrinkles to still iron out."

"I understand and Prince Constantine will meet your bride when the time is right." Mrs. Sivka smiled. "I'm proud of you. Your parents would be proud, too. You deserve every good thing coming, you do."

"But you have to say that, Mrs. Sivka," he said, teasing her gently, forever grateful she'd come out of retirement to help with Tinny after his parents' accident. "You were my nanny, too."

"That I was. And now look at you."

He smiled crookedly. "Good night, Mrs. Sivka."

"Good night, Your Majesty."

Zale left his brother's suite of rooms and headed

to his own, feeling tightness and tension return to his chest.

He felt like he'd ridden a roller coaster of emotions tonight. He didn't like it.

He rarely let his emotions get the better of him. Little ruffled Zale. Virtually nothing got under his skin. But tonight everything about Emmeline had gotten to him. She wasn't the one he'd remembered. She was nothing like the cool ice princess of the past. And tonight she'd managed to turn him inside out.

Not good, he told himself, walking to his own suite of rooms in the next wing.

He wasn't supposed to be emotionally involved with Emmeline. As they both knew, their union wasn't a love match but a carefully orchestrated arrangement with significant financial incentives. Every step of their relationship had been outlined and detailed in the final draft of the seventy-page document they'd sign in the morning.

He could want her, desire her and enjoy her but he couldn't ever forget that their relationship was first, and foremost, business.

Business, he reminded himself sternly, which meant he couldn't allow himself to get distracted, not even by a beautiful face and lush body.

Fortunately Zale was famous for his discipline.

That same discipline ensured success in school, in sport and then as Raguva's sovereign.

Growing up the second of three sons, no one placed pressure on him. No one had particularly high expectations for him. But Zale had high expectations for himself. From a young age he was determined to find his own place in the world, would carve a niche that was uniquely his. And so while his older brother, Stephen VII, Raguva's Crown Prince, had learned the fundamentals of ruling a monarchy, Zale had learned the fundamentals of football.

His older brother would be king one day and Zale would play professional sport.

Zale had been sixteen and attending boarding school in England when nineteen-year-old Stephen, in his second year at Trinity College, had been diagnosed with leukemia. His parents and Tinny had relocated to London to be with Stephen during the grueling chemo and radiation treatments.

For three years Stephen fought hard. For three years he endured horrific pain in hopes that the debilitating treatments would knock the leukemia into remission.

Zale had felt helpless. There was nothing he could do. Not for Stephen. Or his parents. And so he poured himself into his sport, needing a focus, a fight of his own. His self-imposed training regime had been grueling—three, four hours a day—running, weight training, sit-ups, push-ups, sprints, drills. He pushed himself to breaking point each day. He worked to muscle failure. It was the least he could do. Stephen was fighting for his life. Zale should struggle, too.

After passing his exams, Zale made the decision to follow his brother to Oxford, where in his first year he made the university's football club's first team, the Blues.

In his second year he carried the Blues to Oxford's newly created Premier League where they finished top.

Stephen was there for the last big game of their season. He'd insisted on attending and their father, Raguva's king, pushed frail Stephen into the stadium in a wheelchair and no one cheered louder than Stephen during the game.

A week after the game, Stephen had died. Zale blamed himself. The day at the stadium had been too much for Stephen. He shouldn't have gone.

Zale remembered nothing of his final year at Oxford. It was a blur shaped by grief. The only time he felt present in his skin was on the pitch. By the time he graduated, four different football clubs competed to sign him to their team.

He'd signed with a top Spanish club despite his parents disapproval. They had wanted him to return to Raguva—he was the Crown Prince now—but Zale didn't want to be king. He had a love, a passion, a dream. It was football.

Football, Zale silently repeated, entering his suite of four rooms, which had served every Raguvian king for the past five hundred years.

His valet was waiting for him in his dressing room, the King's Dressing Room, where the sumptuous curtains had been drawn across the wall of leaded windows, shutting out the night.

"Was it a good evening, Your Majesty?" his valet asked, assisting Zale out of his formal jacket.

"It was, Armand, thank you." Zale's jaw tightened as he began unbuttoning his vest and dress shirt.

No, he'd never wanted to be king, had no desire to rule, but when his parents' plane had crashed on landing, of course he came home. And he turned his tremendous discipline and drive to his reign.

He'd be a great king.

He owed it to his people, his parents and most of all, Stephen.

Hannah slept fitfully that night, tossing and turning in her ornate bed in her sumptuous bedroom, dreaming of Zale, dreaming of leaving, dreaming of finding Emmeline only to lose her again.

She woke repeatedly during the night to check the clock, anxious about the time, anxious about getting to the airport in the morning. At three she climbed out of bed to push the heavy drapes open, exposing the window with the night sky and quarter moon.

But finally it was dawn and pink and yellow light pierced the horizon. For a moment Hannah lay in bed watching the sun slowly rise, the yellow and pink sky deepening to gold and coral.

It would be a beautiful morning. Not a cloud in sight. There was nothing but soaring green mountains behind the walled city and the Adriatic Sea stretching before.

Hannah left the bed to stand at the window wanting to remember everything.

The rugged mountains. The pale stone houses and walls. The red tile roofs. Church spires and castle turrets. The sparkle of the sun on the water.

This morning Raguva's capital looked magical, as if it had been plucked from a fairy tale.

She felt a tug on her heart and that tug was enough to make her turn away.

She wasn't going to think today. Wasn't going to

feel, either. There would be no remembering last night, not even guilt over that kiss in the corridor.

She was going home. Back to her work and world. Back to a life where she excelled and could make a difference.

But first she'd need to shower, and then she'd dress and pack the few personal things she'd brought with her into an elegant shopping bag she'd found a few days ago.

The shopping bag was part of her "escape" plan. It was really quite a simple plan, too.

She'd make arrangements to go out shopping this morning. A driver could take her to an upscale fashion boutique where she'd window-shop and wait for Emmeline's call. Once Emmeline phoned, Hannah would head to the airport where she and Emmeline would meet in the ladies' room, change into each other's clothes and swap places. Easy.

Once bathed, Hannah searched for a dress in Emmeline's wardrobe that would fit both she and Emmeline. Hannah settled on a plum dress with a jewel neckline and cutout cap sleeves that could be worn with an optional gold belt. Hannah would leave the belt off but take it in her purse so that Emmeline, who was at least ten pounds lighter, could cinch the belt around her waist to keep the dress from looking baggy on her more slender frame.

Hannah pinned her hair up in a casually chic French twist, and added classic gold earrings as her only other accessory. The less she had to put on and off the better.

Once dressed and packed, the only thing Hannah could do was wait. She called for coffee and a footman arrived with coffee and croissants.

Hannah nibbled on a croissant while waiting for Emmeline to call.

A half hour became an hour, and then two and soon it was nine o'clock and Lady Andrea arrived to cover the day's schedule with her.

"It's going to be a very busy day," Lady Andrea said, taking a seat in the suite's sitting room and pulling out her leather calendar to flip to the proper page. "At ten this morning you have an appointment with His Majesty, and the lawyers in His Majesty's chamber, and then at eleven you'll have your hair and makeup done for the first sitting for your official portrait. Later, if there's time after tea, Mr. Krek, the Head Butler, will take you on a tour of the palace. Tonight you'll have a private dinner with His Majesty and a few guests."

Lady Andrea drew a breath and looked up at Hannah. "Any questions?"

A half dozen questions came to mind, but nothing as pressing as the meeting with Zale in just under an hour. "What is the purpose for the meeting with His Majesty and the lawyers?"

Lady Andrea closed the leather appointment book. "You're meeting to sign paperwork, I believe."

Hannah felt an icy rush of panic. "What paperwork?"

"The prenuptial agreement, Your Highness, spelling out division of assets, as well as custodial arrangements, in the event of the dissolution of the marriage."

Hannah's mouth opened and closed. Of course Zale and Emmeline would have a prenup, but Hannah couldn't, wouldn't sign a legal document in Emmeline's name.

Thank God Emmeline was on her way. Only problem was, Hannah didn't know when the princess would arrive.

Hannah stole a quick glance at her watch. Nine-fifteen. The meeting with Zale and the lawyers was only forty minutes from now and even if Emmeline landed right now, it would still be impossible for Emmeline and Hannah to switch places by then.

She'd have to stall. Have to get the meeting postponed until later.

"Could you please send word to His Majesty that I'd like to push back this morning's meeting to this afternoon, or even tomorrow morning?" Hannah said. "I'd like time to review the documents before I sign anything."

Lady Andrea hesitated, then nodded. "Of course, Your Highness, I'll send word to His Majesty's secretary and see if we can't get this morning's meeting rescheduled. I'll also request copies of the documents be sent to you immediately."

As soon as Lady Andrea left, Hannah checked her phone to see if she'd missed a call or text. Nothing.

But why nothing? Hannah pressed two fingers to her temple trying to ease the pressure building in her head.

Where was Emmeline?

Hannah sent her yet another text. *What's happening? Where are you? When will you arrive?*

Phone tightly clutched in her hand, Hannah paced her suite, desperate for a response. Call, call, call, she silently chanted, anxious beyond belief. But minutes crawled by without a word from Emmeline. Five, ten, twenty. And each minute made Hannah more nervous.

Lady Andrea returned, flustered. "Your Highness, His Majesty can't reschedule this morning's meeting. He asked that I remind you that you just approved the document and its contents two weeks ago—"

"I understand," Hannah interrupted, panic sharpening her tone, "but I'm not feeling well enough to meet him—much less sign anything—right now. Please send my apologies—" Hannah broke off as her phone suddenly buzzed. She glanced at her phone. Emmeline.

Thank God. She must have just landed. Everything would be okay. Hannah would just postpone the signing for an hour or two to allow Emmeline to arrive at the palace.

Hannah glanced at Lady Andrea, and smiled weakly. "Please see if we can't reschedule for after lunch. I'm sure my headache will be gone by then."

Hannah didn't even wait for the door to close behind Lady Andrea before reading the Emmeline's text message.

Couldn't get flight plan approved last night—
What? No. *No!*

Tiny spots danced before Hannah's eyes. She swayed on her feet, shocked, sickened. Emmeline hadn't even left Florida yet?

Hannah read the rest of the message with tears of frustration burning her eyes. *Trying to get permission now. Don't panic. Will be there soon! xxx Emme*

Don't panic? She nearly threw her phone across the room. How could she *not* panic?

"No!" Hannah choked, blinking tears, adrenaline making her heart race. "No, no, no!"

She was so furious and frustrated she missed the knock on the outer door, as well as the fact that it had opened.

Hannah might not have heard anyone enter but she felt it immediately, her nape tingling and goose bumps covered her arms. She wasn't alone anymore. Even the energy in the room felt different.

Hannah lifted her head, her fingers stilling about the phone's tiny keypad.

Zale.

And he was upset.

She saw his expression and it took her by surprise.

Why was he so angry? Was it because she had pushed back this morning's signing? But that didn't make sense. Why would rescheduling the meeting upset him so much?

"What's wrong?" she asked, taking a step back.

"What is this about?" he demanded imperiously, approaching her, his handsome features grim, his amber gaze holding hers, commanding her attention.

She sucked in a nervous breath, overwhelmed

by his intensity. Zale Patek hadn't just entered her room, he owned it, dominated it and in turn, dominated her.

Was this the same man who'd kissed her senseless last night?

Was this the man she couldn't bear to leave?

"I don't understand," she said, taking another step back.

Zale kept walking toward her, tension radiating from him in waves. "Neither do I." His tone was clipped, hard. "Explain to me why you've canceled the meeting."

She bumped up against the delicate coffee table between the pink silk sofa and armchairs and had no more room to run. "I woke up with a headache and it's just gotten worse."

"I'm sure you could suffer through for a thirty-minute signing."

"But I can't. The pain's so bad I can't even read right now."

"I'll read it to you, then."

His sarcasm stung. Why was he being awful? Was it necessary to be rude? Necessary to be so inflexible? "I'm sure we can reschedule—"

"No."

"And why not?" she demanded, just as curtly.

He tipped his head, studying her, his short crisp

hair dark, but definitely not black, just as his eyes were neither brown nor gold but a shade somewhere in between. This morning he wore a black suit with a white dress shirt open at the collar. His throat was the same bronze tone as his face. She could almost see him in the sun, his lean, chiseled features glazed by light.

Gladiator.

Warrior.

King.

"Because," he said slowly, clearly, "the lawyers are here, the paperwork is ready and the agreement is to be signed now."

"Even if I don't feel well?"

His features tightened, his mouth compressing. "I should have known the games weren't over."

Her hands knotted. "I'm not playing games—"

"What do you want now? How do you intend to up the stakes? Are you holding out for ten million for each child? What is it this time?"

"That's insane!"

"It is, isn't it? But that's how you play, Emmeline—"

"No. You couldn't be more wrong. I'm not changing anything or asking for anything other than a postponement so I can take some medicine and lie down and try to feel better."

"What's wrong?"

"I told you. I have a headache."

"Is that so?" His deep voice mocked her even as his gaze examined her, slowly scrutinizing her appearance from the top of her head down to her toes.

Hannah could see herself in his eyes—her perfectly coiffed French twist, the rich plum of her dress and the expensive designer shoes. She'd dressed smartly, elegantly, knowing that when she left the palace this morning she needed to look every inch the royal princess.

"Yes," she answered, lifting her chin, staring him in the eye, daring him to call her a liar. She'd been raised by a tough man. Her father didn't tolerate fools, either, but her father had also taught her that men were to be gentlemen. Men were to treat women properly—which meant with kindness and respect. And Zale Patek was definitely not treating her with respect right now. "But if you don't believe me, would you like to call a doctor? Have him examine me? Would that reassure you, Your Majesty?"

"That's not necessary," he said stiffly.

"But I think it is. Clearly you doubt my sincerity. You've questioned my integrity—"

"I haven't."

"You have. You've been rude. Why? For what? A prenup?"

Heat flared in his amber eyes, making them gold. "Your father was the one that wanted the contract. It was drawn up at his insistence and at great expense, so don't put that one on me."

Hannah blanched. The contract had been Emmeline's father's idea? What kind of father was this King William of Brabant? He certainly didn't sound supportive or loving.

"Everyone is here because of you," Zale added tersely. "Five lawyers, Emmeline. Two of whom flew in from your country, and one from overseas, and now I am to tell them to go to their rooms and twiddle their thumbs until the morning?"

He had a point. But what was she to do? Sign as Emmeline? Impossible. "Yes," she said firmly. "That's exactly what you do when your future queen is ill and unable to make the meeting."

Zale drew a slow breath. He exhaled. A small muscle pulled in his jaw.

"I apologize, Your Highness," he said from between clenched teeth, color darkening the high slash of cheekbone. "I did not mean to appear insensitive. Your health is of course my first concern. Everything else can and will wait."

Then with a brief, icy bow, he walked out.

CHAPTER FOUR

HANNAH sank into the nearest chair after Zale left, heart racing so fast she felt like throwing up. For a long moment she couldn't think, too rattled by the intense confrontation with Zale to do anything but process what had just taken place.

He'd been so angry. And his anger had felt personal. As if he was disgusted with her.

Why?

Why would delaying the meeting upset him so much? She hadn't said she wouldn't sign it. She hadn't asked for changes. She'd just asked for time. But it seemed as if time wasn't something Zale was prepared to give her.

And then she remembered something he'd said, spitting the words at her as if they'd hurt his mouth—*I should have known the games weren't over.*

Then he'd added something about her raising the stakes, holding out for millions, because that's how she played.

How *she* played?

He was the one who had burst into her room, temper blazing, words coldly mocking.

I did not mean to appear insensitive. Your health is my first concern. Everything else can wait.

Liar! He didn't mean a word of it. He'd totally meant to be insensitive. He'd been deliberately rude.

From the moment he'd entered her suite he'd shown absolutely no concern for her health. Instead he'd bullied her. Tried to intimidate her. Accused her of playing games.

Who did he think he was, treating a woman like that?

Livid, Hannah chased after Zale, catching up with him as he descended the grand staircase. "Your Majesty, I'd like a word with you," she said sharply, stopping him midstep.

He slowly turned to look up at her, his straight eyebrow lifted in surprise. "Your head seems to be much better."

"It's not," she answered shortly, cheeks flushed, body shaking with tension, "and you owe me an apology. You were unforgivably rude."

"*I* was rude?"

"And cruel. You should be ashamed of yourself! I can't believe that's how your parents raised you."

Color darkened his cheekbones and his eyes glittered with anger. "I could say the same for you. Engaged to me and yet playing the field—"

"How dare you!"

"Save me the theatrics. I know, Emmeline. I know the truth."

"What truth?"

"I know why you were in Palm Beach. I know what you were doing there—"

"Attending fashion shows and dinners and a charity polo match."

"God, you're good," he said, moving back up the stairs with that stealthy animal grace that made her pulse leap and heart beat too fast. "Charity polo match! That's wonderful. Cling to your story. Keep to the facts, right?"

"I have no idea what you're talking about."

"Don't go there," Zale said, joining her at the top of the stairs, and his sheer size and intensity overwhelmed her. She didn't like how he towered over her. Didn't like that she had to tip her head back to see his expression. Being this close made her feel alarmingly vulnerable.

"What does that mean?" she demanded fiercely, her heart racing, her pulse unsteady.

"Emmeline, I *know*. I know why you were in Palm Beach. I know you went to meet him. I know you spent every free moment in Florida you could with him."

Hannah inhaled hard, stunned. Couldn't be... Emmeline couldn't have been with someone else when she was engaged to the King Patek...could she?

"No," she whispered, not wanting to believe it, not wanting to imagine that beautiful, charming Emmeline d'Arcy would be unfaithful. "That's not true."

"Don't add insult to injury! It's bad enough you were seeing him throughout our engagement, but don't lie to me, too. You were seen together—constantly—mutual friends were concerned enough to phone and let me know."

Hannah felt cold. His ugly, hurtful words made her sick. "What friends?" she murmured faintly, horrified that this was the kind of relationship Zale and Emmeline had. How could they marry when they mistrusted each other so? When they had so many secrets? Where was the warmth? And respect?

"Does it matter which friends?" he answered wearily, his expression shuttered. "Because it's the truth. You were with Alejandro every moment you could spare. I wasn't even sure you'd get on the plane to come here."

Hannah laced and unlaced her fingers, heartsick.

That's why Emmeline had wanted Hannah to switch places with her? She'd wanted more time with her lover. No. No, couldn't be…

Was Emmeline that cold? That calculating?

Hannah shook her head, confused, betrayed and wished with all her heart she'd never started this terrible charade. She'd thought it was an innocent prank, pretending to be Emmeline for a few hours, but instead there was so much more at stake.

Countries. Kingdoms.

A man's self-respect.

Hannah's eyes burned and she had to look away to cling to her control. "I'm sorry," she said, thinking the words didn't mean much because they'd change nothing. Emmeline still wasn't here. Hannah was pretending to be someone she wasn't. And the charade continued, making Zale Patek the fool.

Her father would be so ashamed if he saw her now. He'd raised her to be strong, independent and true.

True.

But oh, she wasn't being honest now. She was anything but. And Zale deserved better.

At the very least, he deserved the truth.

"But you did come," he said after a moment, breaking the strained silence. "Do you mean to stay? Or are you just waiting for an opportunity to escape?"

Hannah went hot then cold, lips parting—but what could she say?

Nothing.

So she closed her mouth and just looked at him, heart aching, wanting so badly to tell him everything but not knowing where to start.

And then he turned, jaw hard, tight, and continued on down the stairs, his broad shoulders squared.

Zale needed air. Badly.

He walked through the central hall down a corridor, leaving the beautifully restored palace for his favorite wing—the original castle keep, a stone tower built nearly a thousand years ago with thick walls and a proper parapet for soldiers to patrol.

As a boy this had been his favorite place to hide, a place neither of his brothers could find him and his parents wouldn't dream to go.

On top of the tower he felt free.

He needed that freedom now. Needed freedom to think, freedom to breathe.

Zale walked the parapet with the stunning views of the old medieval walled town nestled between the green slope of mountain and the blue Adriatic Sea.

He'd lost it earlier in Emmeline's room. Completely lost it. And he never did that. At least, he hadn't, not in years.

But oh, dear God, he felt like he was close to losing it again.

He knew there had been issues before she'd arrived. He knew he'd have to make a decision about her, and their future, once he'd spent time with her. But spending time with her didn't help. Spending time with her was making him mad.

Was she crazy, or was he?

How could one woman appear to be so many different things?

She was just so different than he'd expected. She'd always been beautiful, but she'd never been this fierce or strong. But the Emmeline now under his roof was downright fierce. Feisty. Warm. Complex.

He struggled now to remember the princess he'd met at the engagement party a year ago. She still looked like that Emmeline—well, a healthier, more athletic version—and she was still as intelligent and articulate, but everything else was different.

Her expressions.

Her mannerisms.

Her inflection.

Everything had changed since that evening, but he didn't understand it. Didn't understand her.

This was the part that bothered him most.

Which was the real Emmeline? The Emmeline that was so reserved and cool he'd once compared her to a beautiful marble statue—all sleek lines, stunning face and perfect proportions?

Or the warm, engaging, challenging Emmeline here? The Emmeline who blushed easily, spoke quickly and responded to his kiss last night with hot, sensual passion?

Maybe if he was just a man instead of a king, he could choose emotion and passion, but he was a king. And he was responsible for the future of his country.

He needed a proper princess.

He needed the right princess.

And as beautiful as Emmeline was, she didn't appear to be the right princess after all.

While he welcomed passion, he needed suitability.

He needed predictability.

Strength of character.

And the Emmeline that was here appeared strong, but was it real, or an act?

And the fact that he didn't know just nine days before their wedding was a huge red flag.

How could he afford to risk his country's future on an enigma? A question mark?

He couldn't. He wouldn't. But if he was going to end this, then he needed to do it soon. He'd accept the blame, pay the penalty and be free. The longer he put it off, the worse the repercussions would be.

In her suite, Hannah felt positively sick. Anxiously she paced the living room, stomach churning, nerves stretched to breaking.

Zale thought he knew the truth. He thought he knew everything. But he didn't, and Hannah should have told him.

She should have confessed who she really was and asked him to forgive her for her part in the deception and then headed to the airport to get a flight home.

But she hadn't done that. She'd allowed him to walk away thinking that maybe finally everything would be okay.

Hannah was still pacing when Lady Andrea gently knocked on the door and opened it. "Your Highness? Your stylists are here to prepare you for your sitting. Shall we get started?"

Hannah opened her mouth to protest but closed

it, knowing she was in too deep now. And the only way she'd get out of this in one piece was for Emmeline to arrive so Hannah could escape.

"Yes."

Nearly three hours after the clash with Zale, Hannah still sat in a chair before the dressing-room mirror, watching Camille, Emmeline's personal hairstylist for the past seven years, spritz a tiny bit of hairspray on Hannah's hair to discourage fly-away strands.

It was all Hannah could do not to wiggle as Camille ran a light, practiced hand over Hannah's hair, ensuring all the ends hung straight. "No more do-it-yourself color, *oui,* Princess?" she said, tapping her on the shoulder. "If you want to go darker, or put in streaks, next time ask me. *Oui?*"

"Oui," Hannah agreed, thinking at that point she'd agree to anything just to get the marathon session over. She'd wanted a diversion, but two and a half hours in this chair while Camille colored, cut and then blew her hair dry using a large round brush to make it straight and glossy, was just too much. Hannah rarely did anything special with her hair, and was amazed that Emmeline could tolerate having her hair professionally styled every time she stepped out in public.

Teresa, Emmeline's personal makeup artist, had

spent a half hour on her face and she moved forward now as Camille stepped back to apply one last coat of mascara and then another dab of soft gold gloss over Hannah's matte rose lipstick.

"Perfection!" Teresa murmured, nodding approvingly as both she and Camille critically examined their handiwork, looking for any flaws. "What do you think, Your Highness? Anything you'd like changed?"

Hannah forced herself to focus on her reflection. Her hair hung straight and very golden—she'd never been this blond in her life—even as her eyes had been subtly lined and lashes darkened to intensify the blue of her eyes. Her lips were full and a discreet golden pink. Her couture gown—the color somewhere between gold and sand—had a deep V neckline and long straight sleeves making Hannah feel unusually sophisticated.

"Nothing," Hannah answered, astonished by how much she looked like the real Princess Emmeline.

Now that her hair had been cut and colored, with her makeup applied by the same deft hand that did Emmeline's makeup, Hannah truly could pass for the princess.

If she didn't know better, even she would think they were twins. "I look…I look…" She searched for the right words to express herself but couldn't find them.

"Stunning," a deep voice said quietly from the doorway, finishing her sentence for her.

Hannah's hands clenched the arms of her chair as her gaze met Zale's in the mirror. He was no longer angry, just somber, but she wasn't ready to see him. Too much had been said already for one day.

But he lifted a hand, dismissing the stylists. "We'd like some privacy, please."

She swallowed uneasily as they slipped away and the door to the dressing room closed, leaving her alone with him.

For a long moment after the others left he said nothing. "I was wrong," he said, breaking the silence. "I handled the situation this morning badly."

It was the last thing Hannah had expected him to say. "I don't suppose you'd ever cancel a meeting for a headache," she said.

"No."

"Just as I don't suppose you ever let a headache keep you out of a football game."

"Definitely not."

Her lips curved. "You played with pain?"

"My job was to play, not sit on the bench."

She'd expected as much. You didn't become a

star midfielder without pain and sacrifice. "So, no excuses."

"No excuses," he echoed.

At least on this point, her father would agree with him. Her father was tough—physically and mentally—and he'd raised Hannah to be the same. She wasn't allowed to make excuses. *Always do your best,* he'd tell her, *no matter what.*

Not that being here, passing herself off as Emmeline, was her best.

"I can understand why you were so upset with me then," she added carefully. "But I didn't this morning. I thought you were being a bully."

"A bully?"

"An unreasonable one."

He looked startled and then he smiled, a quick smile that made him real and warm and sexy.

But she didn't want to find him sexy. Not if he was Emmeline's.

"Have we made a mistake, Emmeline?"

The quiet question in his deep, softly accented voice shocked her. *"What?"*

"I wonder if we're forcing something we shouldn't."

She looked at him, too stunned to speak.

"It's never been easy between us," he added, leaning against the wall, his big shoulders even broader in the black jacket. His brow furrowed. "I know why I've pushed ahead, but why have you? There are a half dozen eligible royals you could marry right now. You could have your pick of any of them—"

"But I chose to marry you," she interrupted softly, because Emmeline had chosen him, and while Emmeline might not love Zale, she must want to be Queen of Raguva.

"Why?"

"For all the same reasons you chose me—our families approved, our countries would forge a stronger alliance, the next generation would be secure."

He sighed and ran a hand along his jaw. "I wish I could believe you."

She sat up straighter. "Why can't you?"

"Your behavior this past year. The secret weekends with your Argentine boyfriend. The prolonged contract negotiations. Your refusal to spend time with me until now." His broad shoulders shifted. "One of those alone would give me pause, but all three? I'd be a fool to trust you."

She knew he was talking about Emmeline, but at the moment his anger and mistrust felt personal. "You'd be a bigger fool to let me go."

Something flickered in his eyes. "Why would I?"

"Your country has felt the same economic downturn that the rest of Europe has experienced, but you have big plans to turn the economy around, and those plans hinge on me." Hannah was grasping at straws now, trying to piece together an argument based on the articles she'd read online about the impact the royal wedding would have on Raguva—increased tourism, greater financial resources, improved clout and visibility. "Since the announcement of our engagement, Raguva's popularity has skyrocketed. The scenic coast has become the new Riviera, and the public can't get enough about us and the wedding. The telecast of the ceremony will bring millions to your treasury—" She broke off, drew a quick breath. "Are you willing to throw all that away on a whim?"

"It's not a whim. I've been concerned about your suitability for a long time."

"Then why have you let it go this long? The wedding is in just nine days. The lawyers are here—all five of them. And the portrait artist is out there setting up his easel this very moment."

His gaze narrowed. His jaw tightened. He didn't speak for so long that the uncomfortable silence turned into exquisite tension. "I like confidence in women, Emmeline, but you're absolutely brazen. You've flaunted your boyfriend beneath my nose for months and yet you expect me to just ignore my better judgment and marry you anyway?"

Heat washed through her, scorching her cheeks, burning her skin. "There is no boyfriend."

"Emmeline, I know all about Alejandro. You've been together for years."

"But that was before we were engaged. We're not together anymore."

He gave her a cool look, features grim. "So how do you explain the photographs of you and Alejandro at the Palm Beach polo match?"

"You know I attended the match and posed for pictures afterward. It was a charity event and I took pictures with everyone. Why aren't you asking me about the photos I took with the English or Australian teams?"

"Because you're not involved with any of their players."

"But I'm not involved with anyone anymore. I'm here, engaged to you."

"Maybe here in body, but not in spirit."

"You don't know that. You can't say that!" She fought back. The last thing Hannah wanted was to be responsible for Emmeline and Zale's relationship. She hadn't come all this way, or struggled this much, to have Zale break off the engagement here and now. No, if Zale wanted to end the engagement, he had to end it with Emmeline, not with her. And if Emmeline wanted to break things off, then she needed to tell him—in person, which meant she had to get here and sort this out herself.

Princess Emmeline's presence was required. Immediately.

"You see only my faults and none of my strengths," she said.

"Maybe that's because your faults outnumber your strengths."

"So that's that? You've made up your mind, decided our fate, game over?"

"You make it sound like I'm an executioner about to take off your head."

"It feels like it."

"Emmeline!"

She shook her head. "You're not giving me a chance."

"I gave you chances—twelve months of them!"

"But I'm here. I came. Let's play the damn game, Zale!"

"What does that mean?"

"It means we're still early in the match and you're wanting to pick up the ball and walk off the field. But we have nine days until the ceremony, nine days to figure out what's real and what's not. So put the ball down. Give me a chance to play."

"And so what do you suggest?"

"We use this time right now to get to know each other. We make every effort to see if this could work before you make a rushed, and rash, decision."

His expression looked skeptical.

"We commit the next nine days to discovering if we're compatible. If we are, we marry as planned. If we're not, we end this amicably."

"It sounds reasonable except for one thing. We can't cancel the wedding at the eleventh hour, not after everyone has traveled at great effort and expense to be here for the event. It would be a public relations nightmare."

"Five days, and we'll make a decision?"

"Four," he countered. "Four days should be more than sufficient if we use the time wisely. And then if I'm still not happy in four, it's over. Done. No more negotiating. Understand?"

His amber gaze burned into her but Hannah stared straight back, lifting her chin, her expression equally determined. "I understand perfectly, but you should know I'm tough. I play hard. And I'm playing to win."

CHAPTER FIVE

THE moment Zale left the dressing room, Hannah grabbed her phone and tried to call Emmeline.

The call went straight to Emmeline's voice mail.

"You need to get here, Emmeline. Zale is threatening to call the wedding off. Hurry." Hannah hung up just as Lady Andrea appeared.

"Your Highness, Monsieur Boucheron, the artist commissioned to do your portrait, is ready."

Hannah slipped the phone back into the drawer beside her bed before following Lady Andrea to the Queen's drawing room where Monsieur Boucheron had set up his easel.

For the next two hours Hannah sat in the small elegant armless chair holding herself perfectly still as the soft yellow afternoon light illuminated her shoulders and face.

Lady Andrea, Camille and Teresa hovered in the background as the artist sketched. Every now and then Camille or Teresa would move forward to smooth a strand of hair, or apply a dab of powder to Hannah's brow or nose.

But Hannah never moved, or complained, her gaze fixed on a distant point.

Her calm was an act. Beneath her cool, half smile, she felt wild.

What if Emmeline was deliberately delaying her flight to Raguva so she could spend more time with her boyfriend? What if Emmeline's goal all along was to have a long romantic break with this Alejandro?

Hannah's hands clenched in her lap. Please don't let that be the case. Emmeline couldn't be so selfish—

"Maybe a break?" The artist suggested, setting down his paintbrush. "Her Highness looks unhappy. Perhaps it's time for a little stretch?"

Hannah nodded, and hurried to her room to try to call Emmeline again. This time she got through.

"I couldn't understand your message," Emmeline said, answering immediately. "The reception wasn't good and the message was broken up—"

"Are you with Alejandro?" Hannah demanded sharply.

"What?"

"You know, your Argentine boyfriend, a member of the polo team."

Emmeline exhaled hard. "How do you know?"

"Zale. He's not happy. You have to come now. Today. You have to sort this out before it's too late."

"You know I'm trying—"

"No, Emmeline, I don't know you're trying. I actually don't think you're trying very hard at all, because things are falling apart here—"

"Things are falling apart here, too!"

"Zale wants to end the engagement. He doesn't think you're compatible."

"How can he say that? He's never spent time with me!"

"Precisely. If you want to save the marriage, you have to get here quickly, because he's giving us—well, you—just four days to prove to him that you're the right one."

"Even at the soonest, I won't be able to get there before morning, so it's up to you to convince him for the next twenty-four hours that he does want to marry me."

"But, Emmeline, I'm not you!"

"So be yourself. Smooth things over. I know you can."

"Why should I? What have you ever done for me?"

"What do you want me to do?"

Good question. What did Hannah want? She already had the great job and good friends. She liked herself. Liked what she'd accomplished in life. All she really wanted now was to fall in love, but she wasn't going to find her Mr. Right if she was with another woman's man. "I just want you to come here and get me out of this. This is your relationship. Your engagement."

"I know!" Emmeline's voice suddenly broke. "Hannah, I know. But I'm in trouble. And I can't see my way clear yet."

"Do you even want to marry King Patek?"

"Yes," Emmeline said quickly then paused. "No. No, I don't. But I have to. It's what our families want. Zale's father and mine. They worked out an arrangement that essentially forces me into the marriage. If I don't marry Zale, it will cost my father five million euros. If I fail to fulfill my obligations in any way, my family pays."

"So you can't end the engagement."

"No. Not without disgracing my family."

"And what if King Patek breaks off the engagement?"

"If he breaks the engagement without cause, he pays my family two and a half million euros. But if he breaks it off with cause, my family still has to pay him five million."

"Why does he only have to pay half of what your family pays?"

"He's a king. I'm just a princess."

Just a princess, Hannah silently repeated, overwhelmed by this world of nobility, wealth and power.

"So you see why I need you," Emmeline said wearily. "I need you to convince Zale I am right for him and once I get there, I will make it work. I will walk down the aisle, and say my vows, and make him happy."

"Can't you talk to your family about this? Can't you go to your father—"

"No. My father would never understand. Or forgive me. My…parents…they aren't like me. They're very strict. Very old-fashioned. I know they mean well but they already disapprove of me, already view me as if I'm…tainted."

"Tainted? How?"

"Not truly noble."

"But why?"

Silence stretched across the line and it took Hannah a moment to realize that Emmeline was crying.

"Emmeline." Hannah felt for the princess. "It's going to be okay. Things always work out—"

"Not this time, Hannah. This time I lose no matter what happens."

Hannah's brows pulled together. She hated suffering in any form, and Emmeline was clearly suffering. "Don't give up. Stay calm. I'll do my best until you can get here."

"Thank you, Hannah, and I will be there. As soon as I can."

Hannah hung up the phone, exhausted. This was such a mess. An absolute disaster.

And none of this would have happened if Hannah didn't wear her heart on her sleeve.

Her father had always warned her that she was too tenderhearted, that people would—and did—take advantage of her. He'd predicted that one day her lack of backbone would come back to haunt her, and he was right. It'd happened.

A half hour later Lady Andrea entered Hannah's suite expecting to find her dressed and ready for dinner. Instead Hannah lay stretched on her bed using her high-tech phone to do some research on the Internet.

"Your Highness, His Majesty is expecting you in minutes."

Hannah looked up from the screen where she'd been doing a crash course on celebrity gossip so she'd know as much as she could about Emmeline's Argentine boyfriend, Alejandro.

It was just unfortunate that she'd waited until now to learn what she could about Emmeline, but celebrities and royals had never interested her, and growing up without a television or even Internet access, she'd never known such a world existed until she entered high school. But now she wished she'd spent a little more time paying attention to Hollywood celebrities and European royals, particularly the young royals today.

"I know. I'll be ready," she said. "I just need to finish this article and I'll go."

"But you aren't dressed for dinner. Do you even know what you're going to wear?"

"No. You can pick something for me, if you'd like."

Lady Andrea sent Hannah to dinner in a stunning marine blue gown that was loosely gathered at the throat and yet cut away to leave her shoulders and arms bare. Rich blue sapphire teardrops hung from her ears and a matching bracelet circled her wrist.

With her hair softly gathered at her nape and sleek high heels on her feet Hannah felt more glamorous than she ever had before.

They were to have a quiet dinner in the King's Chambers, which were four large rooms strung together. Zale's butler opened the living room door, inviting her in.

"I haven't had the pleasure of meeting you yet,

Your Highness, but I look forward to serving you soon," Mr. Krek said with a formal little bow.

Hannah smiled warmly. "It's good to meet you. I've heard so much about you."

He flushed with pleasure. "I look forward to serving you, Your Highness."

"Thank you, Mr. Krek."

"Now if you'll excuse me, I'll see to your drinks and appetizers."

Hannah watched him walk out and she was alone, and then a moment later, she was not.

She knew the moment Zale entered the room. Felt a frisson of pleasure race down her spine. Turning slowly, Hannah looked over her shoulder.

There he was, Zale Patek, standing in the doorway, dressed in an elegant dinner jacket, crisp shirt and tie. His hair was combed, his jaw freshly shaven.

"Your Majesty," she said, suddenly breathless.

"Your Highness," he answered, allowing his gaze to slowly sweep over her, making her feel as if she was about to become his next favorite plaything. He moved from the doorway and walked toward her. "I like the dress."

Her heart beat double fast. "But not the lady?"

His piercing amber gaze met hers. "I'm still trying to decide."

She lifted a brow, her full lips pursing. "Well, when you've come to a decision, do let me know."

Heat shot through Zale, his body hardening instantaneously. My God, she was good. Interesting. *Clever.*

He was fascinated by the way she carried herself, her wit, her intelligence. She was beautiful and challenging and complex.

He'd fully intended to end it with Emmeline earlier today. He was going to make a clean break, wire the money he'd owe the d'Arcy family to the Bank of Brabant and move on so that he could find someone more suitable.

That's why he'd gone to her in her dressing room. That's why he'd been honest.

Blunt.

But now that she was fighting back, demanding a chance to prove herself worthy, he felt compelled to give her that opportunity.

Not out of any altruistic gesture, of course.

When it came to Emmeline he was appallingly carnal. He might not like her, but she was right—he wanted her. And the intensity of his desire surprised him.

He'd thought her beautiful at their engagement party but he hadn't felt this fierce physical attraction that evening. The truth was he hadn't felt much of anything for her throughout the year. Until now.

But ever since yesterday, whenever he looked at her, he thought of one thing—getting her in his bed, naked beneath him.

He wanted to see her long blond hair tousled about her face, a golden ripple across the pillow.

He wanted to part her thighs as wide as he could and bury himself in her, thrusting deep and hard to make her come.

He wanted to shatter her control and make her fall apart and see if there was perhaps a real woman, a warm woman, underneath the shimmering hair and stunning face.

"We both have busy schedules," he said, "but I'll see if I can't have our appointments and appearances shuffled around to allow us to spend as much time together in the next few days—"

"Four," she interrupted. "You've promised me four starting tomorrow."

"I think that was four, starting today."

"Tomorrow," she insisted firmly. "Today was already half over when we made the agreement."

"Perhaps, but as I intend to spend all our time together, I think you might find four days excessively long, unless you don't think you'll weary of me after morning, noon and night?" His voice trailed off and he shrugged, as if to say it was entirely up to her.

Two bright spots of color burned high in her cheekbones deepening her blue eyes. "I would only weary of you if you were boring." Her full lips curved. "Do you intend to be boring?"

She was outrageous. She should be punished. With his hands, and mouth, and tongue.

His body hardened just thinking of how she'd feel beneath him.

Emmeline glanced around the room, her expression serene. "I'm starving. Do you know when dinner will be served?"

"I'm not so easily distracted," he said, "and a change of subject won't change my intentions."

"And I'm sure you've heard the expression, don't put the cart before the horse?"

He let his gaze travel slowly over her, resting provocatively on her breasts, hips and the juncture of her thighs. "Are you the cart? Or the horse?"

Her chin lifted. "Neither."

Hannah was thrilled when Mr. Krek invited them to dinner, which was served at an intimate round table before the living room's tall gold marble fire-place.

"I knew your English was excellent," Zale said, midway through dinner as the footmen removed one plate only to replace it with another. "But I hadn't realized you spoke it with an American accent. Did you study in the States or have an American tutor?"

She'd read that Zale Patek spoke more languages than any other royal—Spanish, Italian, French, English, Swedish, Turkish, Greek and of course his native language, Raguvian. He was that rare breed of scholar and athlete.

"American tutor," she said, trying to remember if Emmeline had ever studied in the United States but didn't think so. "And you?"

"I was educated in England—sent to boarding school at ten, and then on to university after."

"Why England?"

"Tradition. I attended the same schools as my brother, father, grandfather and great-grandfather."

"When you have children, will your son do the same?"

A slightly mocking note entered his voice. "You mean, *our* son?"

Hannah glanced up, straight into his eyes. They were such a unique color, not exactly brown, not exactly gold. "Yes, ours," she said, blushing as she imagined having Zale's child.

"Our one of two," he added. "The heir and spare. It's all you'd agree to give me, remember?"

Hannah just looked at him.

"Why, Emmeline, were you so adamant that it only be two? You never gave me a proper explanation." His lips curved in a lazy smile that failed to touch his eyes. "We finally have time to talk properly. To discuss all the things you wouldn't discuss this past year. I'd love to know why you insisted we limit our family to two. If we hope to save our relationship, then this is probably the best place to start."

"I don't know."

Zale took her hand, lifted it to his mouth. "Was it your figure you feared losing?"

She tugged her hand back, fingers tingling from the touch. "No!"

"Your freedom then?"

"That's silly."

"Well, it is hard to gallivant about when you're pregnant."

"I don't gallivant, and despite what you might think, I look forward to having a family."

"Just not a large family."

"Yes."

"Why?"

"Personal preference. Why do you want a large one?"

"Because I enjoyed having brothers. Their friendship and companionship meant a great deal to me." His lashes lowered concealing his expression as he toyed with the delicate stem of his wine goblet. "Do you ever think your fear of pregnancy might stem from your mother's death after childbirth?"

Hannah froze, suddenly chilled.

Emmeline's mother had died in childbirth?

But how was that possible? Emmeline's mother, Queen Claire, was alive and well and had just been in Spain on holiday last week.

"My mother is alive," she said numbly, finding the subject too close to home as Hannah's own mother had died in childbirth as well.

"I'm sorry. I should have said your birth mother. You were adopted by your parents, King William and Queen Claire d'Arcy, when you were just six days old."

"How did you find out?" she whispered.

"Your father told me several months ago when we hit that impasse in our contract negotiations. He wanted me to understand that your reluctance to have children wasn't out of selfishness, but probably fear."

"So if my father gave you a reason, why put me through this?" Hannah fought to hang on to her temper.

"I wanted you to tell me."

"Why?"

He was angry now, too. "Because just once I'd like to hear the truth from you. I'd like to know the real you. I don't know who that person is, or what she wants, or what she really feels."

She flinched at the words, *real you,* but wouldn't linger on them.

"You want to know what I think?" she blazed. "I think it's a crime that women still die in childbirth. We can put men on the moon. Create weapons of mass destruction. Produce miracle drugs and design modern hospitals. So why can't we make childbirth safe? How can we allow women to die while creating life?"

"Because we're mortal. Life eventually ends for all of us."

Hannah's father, Jake, had said the same thing regularly while Hannah was growing up. "It's tragic." Her voice dropped, deepening. "Children need their mothers."

"Just as mothers need their children." His broad shoulders shifted uncomfortably. "It broke my mother's heart that she couldn't save my older brother. I heard her say more than once, that she wished she could switch places with Stephen."

"Didn't that hurt you?"

"Stephen was her firstborn. She'd always been close to him."

"Weren't you two close?"

"Not as close as I would have liked. But I was the middle child and my younger brother needed my mother more."

"Where is your younger brother?"

"Here, in the palace."

"Why haven't I met him?"

He hesitated, choosing his words with care. "Constantine has special needs and requires round-the-clock care. He forms attachments easily and doesn't comprehend loss."

Hannah frowned, puzzled. "Are you afraid I'll hurt him?"

"Not deliberately. But in order to protect him, I've decided to wait to introduce you until I know you're staying."

CHAPTER SIX

LATER that night, tucked in bed, Hannah took out her phone and researched the Patek Royal family.

There were dozens of articles online but very few references to the youngest Patek prince, Constantine. Once someone gave his date of birth—he was three years older than Hannah—and another time, he was referred to as the third son, but that was it. To the outside world, Prince Constantine didn't exist.

Hannah could see why Zale would want to protect his brother from the world, but to keep his future wife from meeting his only surviving family? It made Hannah think Zale had no intentions of marrying Emmeline.

Hannah turned off the phone, and then the lamp next to her bed, but couldn't sleep.

Zale wasn't an easy man. He was tough, proud and competitive. And the more she got to know him, the more certain she was that he'd crush Emmeline. Not intentionally, of course, but simply because he didn't understand his own strength.

He'd never win Emmeline's heart by browbeating her, either. He needed to court her. Needed to woo her. Needed to show that he had a softer side, and Hannah knew he did because she saw glimpses of it every now and then. Just not often enough.

It was time Zale exerted himself a little bit. Time he made an effort to win Emmeline over instead of judging her and criticizing her. He might be a king, but he needed to start treating his betrothed like the queen she would be.

Hannah woke early the next morning and rang for Celine to help her dress. "Can you send word to His Majesty that I'd like to meet him?" Hannah asked, stepping from her shower to dress.

Today she chose her own clothes, selecting a pale apricot linen dress from Emmeline's wardrobe paired with a slim-fitting cropped cashmere sweater the same hue. She slipped a gold bangle on her wrist and small gold hoops on her ears, before pulling her hair back in a ponytail. She did her own makeup, keeping it light, and was just finishing applying mascara when word arrived that His Majesty was waiting for her in the family dining room.

Hannah took a deep breath and squared her shoulders as a footman escorted her.

The family dining room was a cozy room on the

second floor. Tall mullioned windows lined the walls and sunlight glazed the glass, casting bright rays across the rich walnut table and illuminating the centerpiece of pink and cream tulips in a crystal vase.

Zale sat at one end of the table reading a stack of newspapers, a cup of espresso at his elbow.

Briefly he lifted his head as she entered the room, his amber gaze sweeping over her. "This is a surprise," he said.

"A pleasant one, I hope," she answered, taking the chair the uniformed footman held for her and smoothing the hem of her crisp linen dress over her knees.

The footman poured her coffee and brought her fresh squeezed orange juice before handing her a small elegant printed menu. Her eyebrows arched. A printed menu for a family meal?

Zale must have been able to read her mind as he said from behind his newspaper, "Chef will make anything you like, but he also offers specialty items every morning based on what he's picked up from the local farmers market."

"How do you know what I was thinking?"

"You're easy to read." He folded the paper and set it down.

"So what am I thinking now?" she asked, stirring milk into her coffee.

Zale studied her for a moment, his expression inscrutable. "You're upset that I won't introduce you to my brother, and you're here to convince me otherwise."

"Not at all," she said, lifting her cup to sip the hot, strong coffee. "I think you're spot-on. Your brother should be protected. Until we are absolutely certain we want to proceed with the wedding, we should be careful. I'd hate to grow fond of your brother only to realize you're not entirely suitable for me."

His eyebrow lifted. "And now *I'm* not suitable?"

She offered the footman a sunny smile as he moved forward to offer her a selection of flaky pastries. She refused the pastries and turned her attention back to Zale. "I thought about what you said last night—about our lack of compatibility—and you might be right."

He shifted in his seat, shoulders becoming broader, expression harder. "Is that so?"

She nodded, took another sip of coffee. "We don't know each other, and the only way you'll know I'm right for you is if I'm myself. So from now on, I'm going to be myself, and hopefully, you'll like the real me. But if you don't, I'd rather go home than marry someone who doesn't enjoy my company."

Zale's brows lowered. "You would reject me?"

She smiled, the same patient smile she gave Sheikh Al-Koury when he gave her another impossible task. "Since we're being completely honest, I admit that I don't want to marry someone I don't like, either."

His lips thinned.

She nodded, as if he'd given a sign of agreement. "I'm really looking forward to the next four days and spending time together. I imagine you have some fun activities planned—" she lifted a finger, holding him off a moment "—activities other than signing documents, sitting for portraits and selecting china patterns."

"Those are all necessary if we're to marry."

"Yes, *if.* But as you made clear yesterday, we don't know that we will. In fact, you're fairly certain we won't. So perhaps selecting a china pattern is a bit presumptuous, never mind a colossal waste of time. Perhaps we should slow down and…date… first."

"Date?"

"Mmm. Lunches. Dinners. Activities that allow us to spend time together in a relaxed and enjoyable manner."

"Is this a joke?"

"No. I definitely wouldn't joke about our future."

Zale stared at her through narrowed lashes, his expression grim. "You're so different from a year ago. You were so quiet at our engagement party. You hardly looked at me. Where has all this *personality* come from?"

Hannah shrugged. "It was always there, just a bit squashed by my parents' disapproval. But my parents aren't marrying you. I am."

"And this entire epiphany came to you last night?"

"Yes. As I lay in bed." She gestured to the footman. "I think I'd like the eggs Florentine and some fresh fruit. Thank you." She lifted her white linen napkin from the table and placed it on her lap. "I thought you'd be pleased by my epiphany but you don't seem happy at all."

He didn't look happy, either. His brow was furrowed, his square chin jutted and he was practically glowering at her from across the table. "I find your attitude a trifle cavalier considering the circumstances. Your parents have invested a great deal of money into our alliance—"

"Five million euros."

A small muscle pulled in his jaw at her interruption. "And I, too, am invested."

"Two and a half million. Because you're a king and more important than I am."

"Emmeline," he growled.

It'd meant to be a warning.

Hannah ignored it. "But that's the reality, isn't it? You are a king and I'm just a princess—"

"Stop."

"It's true. You do have more power. You can afford to be critical. Judgmental. Unforgiving."

"That's not who I am."

"It's how you speak to me. You've told me repeatedly that I'm not suitable." Her shoulders lifted and fell. "So why would I want to marry you? Why would I want to spend my life with a person who treats me like my parents do?"

He leaned back in his chair and for a long moment said nothing and then he shook his head. "I respect your parents, but I'm nothing like them."

"Yet all I've heard from you since I arrived is that I'm a disappointment and you can't wait to get rid of me."

"I also think I've told you you're beautiful a half dozen times."

"But I'd rather you like who I am as a person than appreciate my looks. Beauty fades. Appearances change. It's the inside that matters and that's the part of me you don't like."

"I've never said that."

"Because there isn't anything about me—other than my bloodline and my looks—that you do like."

He fell silent. She knew she'd made a point. She could see it in his eyes and the twist of his lips.

Silence stretched. Zale drew a deep breath and slowly exhaled. "I like you right now," he said after a moment. "I like your candor. I appreciate honesty."

Hannah suppressed the twinge of guilt she felt at his mention of honesty. "Zale, I think there are a lot of things you'd like about me, given the chance to get to know me. I love adventure. I have a great sense of humor. I enjoy traveling and reading and learning about new cultures. But if you keep throwing the past in my face, you'll never get to know any of those things about me."

"It's hard to forget that until last week you were with Alejandro."

"Is that pride speaking?"

"No. It's the realist in me. The one that knows leopards don't change their spots."

"But the realist must also see that I'm here. I asked to join you at breakfast this morning. I want to spend as much time as I can with you—Zale, the man, not the king—over the next few days. But you have to want to be with me, too, because I don't want to marry my father. I want a man that likes me. Enjoys me. And could maybe even one day love me."

Zale stood up, walked across the room, then turned to face her. "Maybe we need to start over," he said quietly. "Wipe the slate clean."

"Can you?"

His broad shoulders shrugged. "I won't know until I try. But let's do what you've suggested. Try to act like a normal couple getting to know each other. We'll spend time together…date."

She smiled at the way he said date. He made it sound foreign and exotic, as if it was something he'd never normally do. "Good. It's the only way we'll know if we really have a chance."

"So let's have our first…*date*…today. I've morning meetings but once they wrap up we'll head out for the rest of the day." He paused, thought a moment and then added, "We'll plan to meet at eleven. Wear something comfortable, bring a sweater and a swimsuit, just in case."

A sweater and a swimsuit? She was immediately curious as to where they were going but didn't ask. "I'll be ready."

* * *

Hannah changed into white linen pants, a blue and white striped knit shirt topped by a navy jacket. It was rather nautical but the most casual thing Hannah could find in Emmeline's elegant wardrobe.

Reluctantly she packed one of Emmeline's two-piece swimsuits, thinking there was no way her curvy figure would be covered by the tiny scraps of material, but Zale had said to bring a suit and so she would.

She headed downstairs at five to eleven to find Zale already waiting for her. She'd expected a car would be waiting outside but discovered a helicopter in the enormous circular driveway instead.

The pilot gave both Hannah and Zale headsets to wear for the flight to reduce noise. The headsets came equipped with microphones but Zale was quiet as they lifted off the palace helipad and flew above the walled city over creamy colored bluffs, cypress pines and hillsides dotted with orange and red tiled houses.

Even with the microphones it would be impossible to really talk above the noise and Hannah didn't mind the silence as it gave her a chance to really see Raguva. It'd been nighttime when she'd arrived and she was fascinated by this jewel-like kingdom on the Dalmatian Coast.

"We're going to my island," Zale said, ten minutes into the flight. "I don't go often, haven't been there in years, but I thought we could both use some downtime away from the palace."

For twenty minutes they flew over sapphire water and the odd sailboat, barge and yacht until several rocky islands appeared below. The islands were almost barren with just a few gnarled trees above jagged cliffs. There were stone ruins on one island, and a simple stone house on another. That's the island they were landing on.

The pilot slowly touched down in a clearing before the house and Zale opened the door, climbed out and helped Hannah out. The pilot handed Zale a leather duffel and they spoke together for a moment before taking off.

Hannah watched the helicopter lift off, blades whirring, leaving them alone on a deserted island in the middle of the Adriatic Sea. "He's coming back for us, right?"

Zale's lips curved in a trace of a smile. "Don't worry. He'll be back before it's dark. But even if he isn't, my security detail has been in the water since midmorning. They've secured the island and they can be here in minutes."

"Do you come here often?" she asked, shouldering her beach tote bag and looking around. The simple farm-style house had thick stone walls, single-pane glass windows and a pale terra-cotta tiled roof.

He shook his head. "Haven't been here in years."

"Why?"

"Haven't had the desire, nor the time."

The sun was now directly overhead and it was hot in the sunlight. Hannah peeled her navy jacket off. "I should have brought shorts or worn a skirt."

"You'll be in your swimsuit soon. We're about to head down to the beach for lunch."

"Is that our picnic lunch?" she asked, gesturing to the small leather duffel.

"Nope. My suit, towels and sunscreen."

"Where's lunch?"

"Hungry?"

"Thirsty."

"Come. Let's go to the beach. Everything's already there."

They walked across the clearing toward the cypress trees and a steep staircase chiseled into the stone cliff.

Hannah followed Zale down the stairs slowly, careful not to trip in her heels. The sun beat down on the top of her head and she grew hotter by the moment. Her elegant sandals were totally impractical for the steep descent and her white trousers grew dusty at the hem. And yet the ocean sparkled far below, the sapphire and turquoise water lapping against ivory sand.

The deep blue water looked impossibly inviting. Hannah couldn't wait to get her feet wet. She loved to swim and looked forward to stretching out in the sun.

Zale waited for her at the bottom of the stairs. He'd taken off his shoes and rolled up his sleeves revealing strong tan forearms. "No more stairs till later."

She slipped off her high-heel sandals, flexing her toes. "Good. That was a little scary."

She'd thought they'd already reached the beach but Zale walked around the corner to another private beach. A large colorful blanket was spread out on the sand with a large basket anchoring one corner, and an ice chest on another.

Zale crouched next to the ice chest and opened the top. "Chef took care of us. Beer, wine, water, juice. What would you like to drink?"

"Beer, please," she said, kneeling down on the blanket, feet blistered and totally parched.

"Beer?"

"I love a cold beer on a hot summer day. Don't you?"

"Yes, but not many women do." He withdrew two chilled bottles and a chilled glass.

"I don't need a glass," she said, waving off the glass and taking one of the opened bottles from him. "How did this all get here?" she asked, gesturing to the basket and ice chest.

"My security detail brought it earlier when they secured the island."

"Is this a family island?"

He unbuttoned his shirt, giving her a tantalizing view of tan, taut skin over sinewy muscle. "No, I bought it back when I played football for a living. I wanted a place far from crowds, paparazzi and overly friendly fans."

Hannah almost licked her lips. He looked incredible. The dense curved muscles of his chest gave way to lean hard abs. "Did you bring your girlfriends here?"

"Just one, and only once. She found it too isolated for her liking."

"So what do you do when you're here?"

"Sleep. Read. Relax."

She sipped her beer. "What do you read?"

"Everything. Novels. Biographies. Histories. Whatever I can get my hands on."

Her lips curved and she settled onto the blanket. "Do you have a favorite author?"

"I do, but I don't think he's writing anymore. Most of his books were published nearly twenty years ago. James Clavell is his name. He wrote *Shogun, Tai-Pan, Noble House*—"

"*King Rat*," she supplied, smiling. "I loved his books. My father introduced me to him. For years I wanted to learn Japanese."

"Did you?"

"No. You couldn't find Japanese language classes in B—" Hannah broke off, realizing she came dangerously close to saying Bandera, her hometown in Texas. She flushed, took a quick sip of her beer. "I learned Spanish and Italian instead."

"You're fluent in both?"

"Yes. You are, too. I read somewhere that you know more languages than any other modern royal. Do languages just come easily to you?"

"I worked at it, the same way I worked at playing football. You don't improve if you don't apply yourself."

"Not everyone is willing to work that hard."

He shrugged, the thin fabric of his shirt clinging to his broad shoulders and outlining his muscles. "I don't mind hard work. Never have."

Hannah bit her lip, liking him more with every moment that passed. Zale was her kind of man—gorgeous, built and brilliant, too. Not fair, she thought breathlessly, far too attracted for her own good.

What she needed was to cool down. "Feel like swimming?" she asked.

"Good idea. It's hot." He pointed along the cliff to an opening in the rock. "There's a little alcove over there by the rock where you can change. Or if you don't like caves, you can just change here, and I promise not to look."

"Cave sounds great," Hannah answered, grabbing her suit and getting to her feet.

In the hollowed-out rock she stripped off her clothes and stepped into the tangerine bikini bottoms before tying the strings of the bikini top around her neck and back. The tiny shiny orange triangles barely covered anything and she sucked in her stomach as if she could somehow make herself smaller.

It took all of her courage to walk back to the blanket in nothing but her suit.

It didn't help that Zale stood at the edge of the water, watching her walk. He'd changed while she was gone and was wearing black and red surfer-style board shorts instead of the traditional European men's suit.

She liked the long board shorts. They hung low on his lean hips, showing off his flat, chiseled stomach. He looked like a surfer—tan, lean, muscular—and she couldn't remember the last time she had found a man this sexy.

Dropping her clothes on the blanket, Hannah walked toward him. "I like your board shorts. Do you surf?"

"I do." He paused. "Well, I did. I grew up surfing—my brother Stephen was really good—but haven't gone on a true surf trip in years."

She waded into the water, gasping a little at the cool temperature. "Where would you go?"

"Wherever there were good waves. Rincon, Brazil, Indonesia, Costa Rica." He ran a hand through his hair, muscles in his thick bicep flexing. "I miss it. But then I miss football, too. I find it hard, being inside, sitting at a desk, as much as I do."

"So how do you handle it?" she asked, wading deeper and sinking down to her shoulders. The water felt warmer already.

"I run and work out. A lot."

There was a roughness in his voice, a sound of pain, and Hannah's chest squeezed. Everything about him was so real, so physical.

Here on this island he was a man, not merely a king, and she found the man incredibly appealing.

Her survival instinct told her to be careful, that allowing herself to feel anything for him would lead to danger. But Zale was so hard to resist. Who else had this combination of dense muscle, burnished skin, keen intellect and burning ambition?

"You need a proper vacation," she said huskily. "A chance to just unplug and unwind."

"It'd be nice."

"Why don't you take one?"

"Our honeymoon was supposed to be one."

Hannah inhaled sharply, feeling as if she'd gotten a kick to the ribs.

She'd forgotten yet again that she was supposed to be Emmeline. Forgot he would soon marry Emmeline. Would soon honeymoon with her.

The thought of Zale with Emmeline hurt. "Remind me, what are we doing for our honeymoon?" she asked, hating that she already felt jealous. Hating the idea of them together on a beach like this, talking like this…

"We're spending ten days on my yacht in Greece and then a few days in Paris so you can do some shopping."

Hannah chewed on her inner lip, thinking that Zale did not strike her as the type to enjoy cruising the Greek islands on a yacht. He struck her as too active for ten days of sunbathing on a yacht. Some rest was good but wouldn't he also want adventure, or some of an adrenaline rush? "That doesn't sound fun for you."

"It's what you wanted."

He meant, that was what Emmeline wanted.

Hannah shook her head, unaccountably angry. Emmeline and Zale were not a good fit. They didn't belong together. Emmeline didn't even want to marry him but was doing it out of obligation. How could this be a happy marriage?

But Hannah couldn't say anything. It wasn't her place to say anything. She was just here as a place-holder until Emmeline arrived.

And even that made Hannah furious.

She dived under a wave, exhaled until she needed air and then popped back to the surface. Still upset, she swam a few strokes before turning on her back to float. The sun shone brightly overhead. The water felt cool against her skin and she could taste the tang of salt on her lips.

Zale was not hers.

Zale would never be hers.

She had to remember that. Couldn't forget it. Couldn't let personal feelings cloud the commitment she'd made to Emmeline. Even if that commitment made her heart ache.

Hannah turned onto her stomach and swam

slowly back to the beach where Zale sat on the sand waiting for her.

"You're a good swimmer," he said as she walked out of the water. His gaze was warm as it slowly swept over her, lingering on the small triangles that barely covered her full breasts as well as the scrap of fabric between her thighs.

She could tell from his expression that he liked what he saw and it made her nipples harden and thrust against the wet flimsy fabric of her bikini top.

Nervous, she slicked her long wet hair back from her face. "I love the ocean," she said, her legs feeling strangely weak. No man had ever looked at her like this. No man had ever made her feel special or beautiful. As if she were something to be touched...tasted... "Love being in the water."

"I like watching you."

His voice had dropped, deepened and she felt something coil deep in her belly. Nerves. Adrenaline.

She was wanting all kinds of things she never thought about. Wanting emotions and sensation she never felt.

"Well, I'd love to watch you surf one day," she answered, sitting down next to him. He was so close she could reach out and brush her fingers across his hard bronzed biceps, so close she could see every shadow and hollow of his flat ripped abs.

She wondered what his skin would feel like if she touched him. Wondered what he'd do.

Her fingers curled into a fist. She couldn't think like this. Couldn't be tempted.

"We'll have to plan a surf trip," he said, reaching out to lift her wet hair and twist the long strands, wringing water from the ends. "Where should we go? Bali? Perth? Durban?"

She shivered with pleasure as his warm fingers grazed her shoulder. She liked the way he twisted her hair, the tug on her scalp, the heat in his eyes.

He made her feel beautiful. Desirable.

Hungry.

She touched her tongue to her upper lip, dazed by the need to be touched. She craved his hands on her body, wanted his palms on her breasts.

"Anywhere," she whispered, her breasts aching, her nipples pressing in blatant invitation against her bikini top.

His gaze dropped to her breasts and she could feel the heat in his eyes as if he'd actually caressed her.

"What would you do while I surfed?" he asked,

pushing her back against the sand to straddle her hips.

He was hard and she gasped, looking up into his eyes, her lips parting helplessly. It felt so good. She wanted more of him and was aching for him to touch her.

"I couldn't just leave you at the hotel bored," he added, reaching out to cup her breast, fascinated by her response.

"Wouldn't be bored," she choked, her voice failing her, her inner thighs squeezing tight as hot sensation rushed through her. She wanted him between her thighs, his mouth on her nipple, his hands stroking everywhere…

"What would you do?" he asked.

She could hardly think straight. "Read."

"I don't know if that would work," he murmured, slipping a hand into her thick wet hair, and drawing her head back so he could see her face.

"Why not?"

Desire burned in his eyes, formed lines at his mouth. A rich dusky color warmed his cheekbones. "I don't know if I could leave you alone long enough to go surf. I don't think I'd want to surf, not if I had you in my bed."

She just stared up into his eyes, lost in him.

He stretched out over her, bracing his weight on

his elbows and lowered his head to touch his lips to the tender skin beneath her pale jaw. "I want you."

He'd only brushed his lips against her jaw in the most fleeting of touches and yet the place he'd kissed burned, her skin too hot and sensitive.

"But you know that, don't you?" he added, kissing yet another spot, making her nerves dance. "You know I can't stay away from you even when I should."

She shivered helplessly as his mouth melted her defenses, turning her inside out. She couldn't even focus on what he was saying, not when his lips were making her body ache for him.

"And yet I should," he added, voice pitched seductively low. "At least until we both know what we want."

Hannah quivered as his voice rumbled through her, making her squirm. She knew what she wanted. She wanted him. Zale. Wanted to wrap herself around him and never let go.

He pressed another kiss to the base of her throat before turning her over, pulling her on top of him. Gritty sand slipped between them. The sun shone hotly, but nothing was as hot as Hannah's hunger as he put his hands on her waist, sliding one hand down across her bottom while the other slid up to cup her breast.

His hands were so warm and they made her feel as if she were on fire. She ached and tingled and burned, shivering against him.

"I think I know what I want," she breathed, as his thumb found her taut, aching nipple and strummed it. "But maybe that's not what you're talking about."

"And what do you want?"

She could hardly think straight, wasn't even sure where she was or what was happening, only that she wanted more—more him, more skin, more sensation. "You."

"But for how long?" he asked, kissing the side of her neck and then brushing his lips over hers.

She kissed him back, lifting an arm and clasping the back of his neck. He was so tall, so hard, so strong. She was safe with him. He'd never let anyone hurt her. "For ever," she whispered against his mouth, not caring if he heard her, not caring about anything anymore but him.

When would she ever meet someone like Zale Patek again? When would she ever feel so alive and beautiful again?

He lifted his head to look into her eyes. His eyes were dark, his cheekbones jutted, his expression intense. He looked wild. Fierce. Primal.

"Be careful what you say," he murmured, molding her nearly naked body even closer to his. She could feel his warm skin against hers and his hard shaft press against her belly.

He cupped her backside in his hands, holding her hips firmly against him, making her gasp as he rubbed her over the head of his shaft once and again.

She could feel the thickness and length of his erection through his board shorts. Felt the corded muscles of his thighs and the thick muscles in his back. He was gorgeous, so very, very gorgeous. "I do want you," she said, her voice breaking. "Even if it's wrong."

His head dipped, his lips taking hers in a slow, deep, bone-melting kiss. "I can't make love to you now," he said, his voice hoarse in her ear. "But if you still feel this way tonight, Emmeline, you won't be able to keep me out of your bed."

CHAPTER SEVEN

"Why won't you make love now?" Hannah asked dizzily, hands pressed to Zale's warm bare chest. The sun beat down on her back and Zale felt so good, his skin smooth and firm, the scent of him addictive, almost as addictive as his kiss.

His hands rested on her backside, his touch sending rivulets of pleasure through her.

"I don't want to take advantage of you."

Beneath her palms she felt the steady beating of his heart. "You think I'll regret it?"

"Possibly. And I'd hate it if that happened."

"Smart," she answered, voice husky. She sat up, disappointed. But she knew he was right. She probably would have regretted it. Obviously he had more control than she did.

He sat up, caught the back of her head and kissed her head. "Don't look so hurt." His voice was pitched so deep it rumbled through her. "I'm trying to protect you, Emmeline. But it's not easy doing the right thing."

She nodded and stood up, backed away a step, unsteady on her feet. "I understand," she said, horribly close to tears. She liked Zale so much. Wanted him even more.

Zale stood and brushed the sand off, his expression equally grim. "Shall we see what Chef packed us for lunch?"

"Yes," she answered, going to retrieve her towel to wrap around her waist.

They sat in the middle of the blanket and Zale opened the hamper. Hannah watched, her head thick, senses drugged. If his kisses were this potent, Hannah couldn't even imagine how she'd feel if they had sex.

Zale unpacked the lunch hamper in silence and Hannah was good with that. She didn't think she could make small talk, not when her emotions felt so wild. How could she be falling for Zale this hard? How could she want him this much, even when she knew he belonged to Emmeline?

Her conscience felt stricken and yet there was something else primal fighting with her guilt.

Need.

Desire.

And the desire was so foreign to her. She never wanted a man like this. Hadn't needed a man in years.

"I'll let you help yourself," Zale said, handing her a plate.

Hannah looked at all the food Zale's chef had sent—roast chicken, baguettes, cheeses, potato salad, beet salad, fruit and more—but her appetite was nonexistent.

"Would *you* have regretted making love?" she asked abruptly, looking across at him.

Zale sighed. "You have an amazing body and I'd have no problem taking you, exploring you. But… considering there are still serious decisions to be made, I don't think we can just jump into bed."

"So you're still trying to make up your mind about me."

He hesitated, then nodded.

Hannah clenched her hands together. "Forgetting the past, what worries you most about me?"

He looked off into the distance, his narrowed gaze fixed on a distant point out at sea and then his shoulders shifted. "You're just so different, Emmeline. You're not the woman I thought I was marrying. And I don't understand what's changed."

Hannah's heart sank. "You don't like…me?"

"No, I do like you. I very much like the woman that is here on the beach right now. You're smart, playful, confident and sexy. But that wasn't the woman I proposed to a year ago. And that concerns me. People don't change this much. Not at our age."

"Would you feel better if I was more like the old me?"

"Maybe. Probably. I'd at least be on familiar ground."

Hannah mustered a smile even though she felt like crying. "Then I'll work on getting the old me back. Hopefully it won't take long."

They returned to the palace midafternoon after more swimming and sunbathing but there was tension between them and Hannah felt the strain. She was glad when the helicopter arrived to take them back to the palace and told herself she was glad when Zale let her walk away from him and return to her suite of rooms.

She wasn't glad, though.

She didn't want to be alone in her rooms. She wanted to be with him. Wanted what they'd had for a moment on the beach—tenderness, closeness, passion.

Hannah paced her living room absolutely desperate. She'd agreed to play pretend and it was killing her. She wanted to tell Zale who she was, wanted him to know the truth about her, but she knew once she told him, she'd lose him altogether.

It wasn't fair that the one man she wanted most in the world was the one man she couldn't have.

If only she really was Emmeline d'Arcy. If only she could be the princess he needed.

A soft, muffled sound reached her and Hannah paused in the middle of her suite to listen.

There it was again, a low cry—part whimper, part moan—and it sounded as though it were coming from her adjoining bedroom.

Hannah stiffened, her skin prickling. She was about to call for the palace guard when she heard the word *Mari,* Raguvian for Mama.

And then again.

Someone was crying for his mother.

Timidly she went to her bedroom door and pushed it slightly open. Light spilled into the dark bedroom. She could hear the sound of crying more clearly.

Mama, Mama.

Hannah pushed the door all the way open and the light from the living room illuminated the bedroom. She could see all the way across the large room. And although the far corners remained shadowy, she saw a figure in one sitting on the floor, hunched over.

The figure rocked in the corner. "Mama?" he said, slowly lifting his head.

It was a child's voice coming from an adult body, and Hannah knew immediately who was it was. Dark brown hair, sloped shoulders, knees bent and held tightly against his body.

Prince Constantine.

"Tinny?" she whispered, not wanting to startle him.

He scrubbed his face with his forearm and looked at her hopefully. "Mama, home?"

For a moment Hannah couldn't breathe and her eyes burned with tears. She slowly crouched down in the doorway. "No, my love, your mama isn't home." And suddenly her heart felt as if it would break. Mothers needed their children. Children needed their mothers. But it didn't always work out that way. "Do you want to find Zale? I bet he'd like to see you."

"Zale," Tinny said. "My brother."

"That's right. Let's find Zale, shall we?"

Hannah called for a footman, and the footman summoned Mrs. Sivka since His Majesty couldn't be located.

Hannah was sitting with Tinny on the love seat in her living room looking at pictures in a magazine with him when a knock sounded on her door.

Hannah opened the door to a short, round woman in her late seventies. "Forgive me for intruding,

Your Royal Highness, but I understand my missing boy is here."

"Yes, I found Prince Constantine in my bedroom." Hannah opened the door wider, inviting the woman in. "Although I don't know why he was there."

"These are the Queen's Chambers, Your Highness."

Hannah stared blankly at the elderly woman before it hit her. This was his mother's room. The prince came here looking for her. "He still misses her."

The woman smiled sadly. "He doesn't understand why she hasn't come back."

"He knows Zale, though—" Hannah broke off, corrected herself. "His Majesty. We talked about him."

"Prince Constantine adores his big brother." The elderly woman looked at Hannah closely. "And I'm sure you hear this often, Your Highness, but you're the spitting image of your mother."

Hannah's breath caught in her throat. "How do you know?"

"I knew her." She frowned. "My goodness, I don't think I even introduced myself. I am Mrs. Sivka. I'm His Majesty's nanny."

"His Majesty? Zale Patek?"

"The very same. I took care of all the Patek princes as babies, and am back again taking care of Prince Constantine now that his parents are gone."

Hannah gestured toward the couch. "Please, sit. I'd love to hear more about the royal family, about His Majesty as a boy. What was he like? Did he get into trouble?"

Mrs. Sivka's round face creased with a broad smile. "Yes, he did, but then all boys get into trouble, and Prince Stephen and Prince Zale were no exception. They were bright, energetic, mischievous children, eager for adventures and busy planning pranks. Prince Stephen was not as sly as Prince Zale and would get caught red-handed, but His Majesty was small and fast and far more sneaky."

"Small, fast and sneaky, Mrs. Sivka?" It was Zale, and he'd entered the room so quietly that neither Hannah nor the nanny had heard him come in. "That hardly sounds flattering."

Mrs. Sivka's round face was wreathed in smiles. "You were a scamp, Your Majesty, but a very, dear, sweet one."

Zale rolled his eyes and moved to crouch before his brother, Zale's powerful thighs corded with muscles, his evening jacket stretched tight across his back. "Tinny," he said sternly, hands on his brother's knees. "You can't run away from Mrs. Daum. You gave her quite a scare. She's very upset."

Tinny pressed a hand to his mouth, eyes wide. "Playing, Zale. Tinny playing."

"I know you like to play, but you can't just leave her like that. She's crying."

"Tinny love Mmm Daum."

"I know you do. So you can't just go on your own. You must take Mrs. Daum or Mrs. Sivka with you when you want to go for a walk or come see me."

Tinny's dark brown eyes filled with tears. "Tinny see Mama. Tinny miss Mama."

Zale swallowed hard. His voice dropped, deepening. "I know you do, Tinny. I miss Mama, too."

Tinny wiped tears away with the back of his wrist. "Bed now. Story."

Zale nodded and patted his brother's knee. "Yes, let's get you to bed and we'll read you a story. Okay?"

Mrs. Sivka held Tinny's hand as they walked back to his suite. Zale and Hannah followed. Tinny was babbling to himself, and rocking back and forth as he walked.

"It takes him a while to calm down once he's upset," Zale said to Hannah.

"He still misses your mother."

Zale's expression was troubled. "It's hard, because there's nothing I can do. There's no way I can fix this. He was so attached to my mother, and she was very devoted to him. She spent nearly all of her time with him."

"How did he get to my room?"

"He slipped away from Mrs. Daum while they were out walking after dinner. There are hundreds of hidden doors and secret passage ways in the palace and when he disappeared, Mrs. Daum went one way, my brother went another and panic ensued."

"Does he go to the Queen's Chambers often?"

"He used to, but hasn't in almost a year. That's why no one went there first."

They'd reached Tinny's suite and Zale offered to help get his brother changed into his pajamas, but Mrs. Sivka refused, saying she thought His Majesty and Her Highness should spend the time together. "Once all the guests arrive for the wedding, you won't have time to be alone, so take advantage of the time now."

Hannah hugged Prince Constantine. "Good night, Tinny," she said in Raguvian, kissing his cheek. "Sleep tight," she added in English.

Tinny squeezed her hard. "Night, Em-mie."

Emmie. Such a sweet nickname for Princess Emmeline. Hannah fought the lump in her throat.

Zale was saying good-night to his brother now, and Hannah turned to Mrs. Sivka, her emotions raw. "You're absolutely wonderful, Mrs. Sivka," she said huskily, tears not far off. "I'm so glad I got to meet you tonight, and I think His Majesty was very lucky to have you as his nanny."

"I still think of him as mine," the nanny answered quietly. "They are my boys, even if they are now men." She hesitated, her gaze searching Hannah's. "Are you settling in all right, Your Highness? Is everything to your liking?"

"Everything is wonderful, thank you."

"I understand you visited His Majesty's island today. It was a good day to go to the beach."

"It was. A beautiful day. But then everything has been lovely here, and everyone has been so kind."

"Do you think you could be happy here?"

"I do."

"And His Majesty? Is he being good to you?"

Hannah shot Zale a swift glance. She couldn't help but notice he was listening. Of course he'd listen now. "He's trying," she said, lips twitching.

"I think it's time to separate the two of you," he interjected, taking Hannah's hand in his. "Come,

Emmeline. And good night, Mrs. Sivka, I'll see you in the morning."

Still holding hands, Zale and Hannah walked back to the grand staircase and across to the other wing. Hannah loved the feel of Zale's large, strong hand against hers, his fingers intertwined. It was such a small thing to hold hands, not at all sexual, but rather loving and tender, which is maybe why it felt so special to Hannah. With Zale like this, she felt completely happy. Completely herself.

"Mrs. Sivka said that my rooms are the Queen's Chambers," Hannah said as they turned the corner and walked down the elegant corridor that led to her suite.

"They are," Zale answered, nodding acknowledgment to a palace guard stationed in the hall.

"But why would the Queen's Chambers be so far from the King's? Your rooms are in Tinny's wing, which is a good walk from here."

"Not all kings wanted their queens next door," Zale said, reaching her suite's outer door.

"Because the kings had lovers?"

"Possibly. But there's another explanation."

"What's that?"

"Not all kings liked their queens." Zale leaned past her, opened her door for her.

"Sounds like a common theme around here."

He released her hand but didn't move very far back. "Not to be completely contradictory, but I'm beginning to like you."

Her heart did a funny little jump. "How horrifying for you."

"I know," he answered dryly. "It complicates things."

"How so?"

His lashes lowered and his gaze moved slowly across her face. "I won't want you to go if I really like you."

Heat rushed to her cheeks. Her skin suddenly tingled. "But you don't *really* like me yet."

He looked down into her eyes, heat in his eyes, his expression intense. "I wouldn't be so sure, Your Highness. You've begun to grow on me."

Her pulse raced and her stomach did wild flips. "Heavens," she murmured, her heart suddenly so full it'd begun to hurt, "what a disaster."

"My sentiments exactly." And yet his voice was deep and rough, a sexy rumble of sound that made her feel absolutely breathless.

Hannah was falling for him, falling hard and fast. "Do you want to come in?"

"It's late—"

"Not that late. Just ten now. We could ring for coffee or a glass of port."

He gave her a long look. "If I came in, I wouldn't want coffee."

Blood rushed to her cheeks and her belly tightened, her body feeling impossibly hot. "We could just talk."

"You know we wouldn't." His gaze dropped, rested on her mouth, as if imagining the feel of it against his own. "If I had you behind closed doors I'd do what I've wanted to do since the night you arrived."

She struggled to breathe. "And what is that?"

"I'm trying hard to remain controlled here."

"I'm just curious."

"And you know what curiosity did to the cat."

She locked her knees, her inner thighs clenched tight. "Yes, but did it feel good?"

A light blazed in his eyes. His jaw thickened. Stark hunger hardened, was etched across his face. "So damn good," he said thickly, reaching for her, and pulling her to him.

She tipped her head back. "So it was pleasure that killed the cat?"

"You are impossible." His voice was a rasp of sound. "And completely irresistible. If you're not very careful, I'll strip you right here in the hall and kiss every inch of you."

She shuddered against him, desire making her

womb ache. She wanted him. Needed him. "That might be too much of a show for your palace security."

He drew a rough breath, color warming his cheekbones. "You are testing my resolve."

He was so hard and warm and his body felt amazing against hers. She pressed herself to him, rubbed like a cat against him. "You feel so good."

He was gritting his teeth, strain evident on his face. "Can't do this here. Won't. It'd feel wrong in my mother's room."

"Then let me come to yours."

He gazed down into her eyes. "You're serious?"

She nodded. "I want this… I want you."

"Wait one hour. Cool down. Think it through. Because once we do this, once we make love, there's no going back."

CHAPTER EIGHT

HANNAH entered the King's Bedchamber wearing a black coat over her nightgown and black velvet slippers on her feet. She tried to act nonchalant as she walked through the bedroom door even though butterflies were flitting wildly in her middle, making her heart beat too fast.

She saw Zale immediately, barefoot at the far end of the ornate chamber and her stomach flipped all over again. He'd shed his dark jacket, and had unbuttoned his white shirt at the collar and rolled the crisp sleeves back on his tan forearms.

"Brave girl," Zale said from the far end of the chamber where he stood before one of two gold marble fireplaces anchoring the room, and it was a magnificent room, the high ceiling covered in rich paneled wood and Flemish tapestries hung on the dark paneled walls.

But nothing was more awe-inspiring than the enormous canopied bed that dominated the room. The bed was huge, bigger than an American king-size—obviously designed for true nobility.

Gold and brilliant blue fabric draped the numerous windows, warming the chamber and shutting out the night while thick blue velvet lined in gold hung from the bed frame, creating an intimate cocoon inside.

"You're here," he said, hands on his hips, studying her from beneath lowered lashes.

Not so brave, she thought, feeling as if she'd entered the lion's lair, with the lights dimmed and the bed prepared for seduction.

Hannah glanced once again at the immense bed, seeing how the brocade coverlet had been turned down, revealing pristine white sheets and pillows. For centuries powerful kings had slept, dreamed and prayed there. And soon she'd be in it, too.

She licked impossibly dry lips. "I am."

"And you've carefully thought this through?" His eyes met hers and held.

The room glowed in the soft candlelight, creating dancing shadows and Hannah plunged her hands into the deep pockets of her coat, self-conscious that Zale was still dressed and she had nothing on underneath her coat but the thin nightgown. "I have."

His lips curved and he began to unbutton the rest of the buttons on his crisp white dress shirt one at a time. "Then why stand so far away?"

But her feet wouldn't move. She was rooted to the spot, mesmerized by his long, lean fingers unfastening the small buttons on his shirt.

Was he really undressing before her?

Was she really going to do this? Then he shrugged out of the shirt, revealing bronzed skin over dense, sinewy muscle, and her mind went blank.

God, he was beautiful.

With perfect aim he tossed the shirt onto the back of a nearby chair. "Second thoughts?"

She shook her head, touched her tongue to her lips again. "No."

"Then come." He curled a finger, beckoning her, thick bicep curving.

He had an amazing body, an athlete's body with broad shoulders, deep chest and hard flat abs that tapered to narrow muscular hips, a body that had taken years to develop.

"Come," he repeated. "I'm hungry for you."

Hannah shivered at the rough urgency of his voice and the sexy command, *Come. I'm hungry for you.*

For a moment her conscience shrieked a protest, and then she silenced it. She needed him. Needed this.

It'd been forever since she'd been wanted, forever since anyone had touched her, loved her. And it was hard to pretend she never needed anything, much less love.

Not that this would be love.

But it'd be something. Zale liked her. Wanted her. And for tonight that was enough.

Hannah walked toward him. She felt his gaze travel over her face and down her body as she closed the gap between him, her breasts growing heavier and more sensitive with every step until she stood before him. He was tall, very tall, and muscular, and overwhelmingly male.

He reached out and unknotted the sash on her trench coat and discarded it. And then watching her from beneath heavy lids, he pushed the coat back from her slim shoulders and let it fall. His gaze dropped to the daring décolleté of her satin gown, the ivory fabric molded to her rounded breasts. Her nipples strained against the satin cups, the darker areola visible through the fabric.

"You are without doubt the most beautiful woman I have ever seen."

His voice was deep, rough with desire and she warmed all over, senses coming to life.

"Beauty isn't everything," she murmured.

A small muscle pulled at his jaw. "You're right." He ran the back of his fingers across her soft cheek. "So what does matter, Emmeline?"

She stared up into his face, seeing emotion darken his eyes and tighten his strong, handsome features. Tension rippled through him. "You. Me. Us."

His gaze dropped to rest on her mouth, his dense black lashes fanning his high cheekbones. "So you know I'm now playing for keeps."

Her cheeks burned, her body felt feverish. She cared about nothing right now but him, this. The future wasn't hers to have. All she had was tonight. All she had was now. "Good."

She took a step closer to Zale and placed her hands on his chest, slowly sliding her palms over the smooth, hard plane of muscle there.

"Make me forget everything," she whispered, voice breaking, as she lifted her mouth to his. "Make me forget everything but you."

Zale slid the straps of her nightgown down over her arms until it fell off her, pooling in a puddle of ivory silk at her feet.

He stood back and looked her over as the fire crackled and burned, light flickering over her, highlighting her curves before slowly drawing her into his arms.

He kissed her as if she tasted like wine and honey, his lips parting hers, his tongue probing her mouth and then teasing her tongue before sucking on it.

She kissed him back, wrapping her arms around

his neck, but even then she felt as if she couldn't get close enough. She wanted more of him, wanted all of him, and she welcomed his hard chest crushing her breasts and the cool buckle of his belt grazing her naked belly.

"Want you," he said thickly.

She nodded and reached for his belt, unfastening the buckle, and then the button on his trousers and finally the zipper.

But before she could tug at his trousers he broke away, leaned over to remove his shoes, socks and then the pants fell, leaving just his snug briefs that barely contained him.

She found herself staring wide-eyed as he peeled the briefs away and he sprung free, very large, very hard and very erect. This king came well-equipped, she thought breathlessly, feeling a pinch of panic as it had been a long time since she'd done this and he looked maybe too big.

"You look nervous," he said.

Her head spun and she moistened her lips. "I am."

"Why?"

"You're…big. Not sure how this will work."

"Don't worry. I know how."

She heard the wicked note in his voice as well as the hint of something else, something that sounded like tenderness.

He took her hand, and tugged, drawing her to the carpet in front of the fire.

She glanced at the fire. "Not the bed?" Her voice wobbled with a fit of nerves. It'd been four years since she made love. Four years before she'd been intimate like this and suddenly she wasn't sure she could do it.

He pressed her gently back onto the carpet, and stretched out next to her, running his hand from her waist, over her ribs, across a full breast and down again. "Love your breasts," he murmured. "They're absolutely perfect."

He stroked her up and down again, his fingers each time brushing lower across her belly until he was caressing the top of her thigh to collarbone and back. She stirred restlessly beneath his hand, arching helplessly as he brushed her curls between her thighs.

"Beautiful," he said under his breath, moving over her, his mouth claiming hers, his weight braced on his arms.

He kissed her deeply, hands still caressing as his knees parted her own. He held her knees apart and then he shifted his weight, turning to press his mouth to her flat belly, his tongue flicking her navel and then lower, his lips brushing across her soft inner thighs and then the softer folds.

She groaned and clenched her hands at her sides, overwhelmed by the intense pleasure.

Zale's tongue traced her tender lips then stroked the tip of his tongue across her tight, engorged clitoris.

She bucked against him when he did it again.

Holding her hips securely, he licked and sucked her wet pink flesh, devoting excruciating attention to her.

Panting, Hannah fought against the hot, sharp sensation building inside her. She'd never done this before, had never been intimate this way with anyone.

But the more she resisted the pressure, the more intense it became. "No," she choked, shaking her head, her legs trembling violently.

"Come on," he said hoarsely. "Come for me."

She heard him, and she knew what he wanted but she didn't think she could it do, didn't think she could just let go, but when he slipped a finger inside her as he sucked, she shattered against his mouth, screaming his name. For an endless moment Hannah tumbled blindly, wildly through time and space, sensations too intense, her body beyond her control.

She was exhausted after, her body tingling and sensitive. She felt utterly spent, and didn't think she could ever want anything again, but when Zale moved over her, and drew a nipple into his mouth, lathing it with attention, fresh desire coiled inside her belly, making her want him again.

He shifted between her thighs but he didn't enter her right away. Instead he sucked and nipped on one pert nipple and then the other, making her grind her hips up against his.

It wasn't long before she was straining against him, desperate to be filled. "Zale." She groaned his name, feeling the thick tip of his shaft brush against her wetness. "Please."

He entered her with a deep, slow thrust and air caught in Hannah's throat. Even though her body was slick and ready for him, he was still big, still stretched her.

She struggled to catch her breath, wanting to relax, wanting it to be comfortable. He eased out and then moved forward again, sliding deeper this time. Again and again he withdrew only to return, deeper, harder and all of a sudden the tension turned to stunning pleasure. She wanted more, wanted him to keep thrusting, craving that intense sensation that told her she was on her way to another orgasm.

"More," she panted, hot, flushed, skin growing damp. "More."

His gaze found hers, held as he quickened his tempo, driving deep into her. She was breathing in little gasps now, shallow breaths as the pleasure built, tighter, sharper, the peak of the climax just out of reach.

"Come," he said, dropping his head to kiss her, and frantically she drew his tongue into her mouth even as he filled her all the way, his body possessing her completely. And just when she thought she couldn't come, that it was too elusive this time, she did, breaking, crashing, her world spinning out of control as she cried his name, again, in pleasure so intense it felt almost like pain.

He came then, in a last deep thrust, his body rigid, muscles tense. She felt his release, felt him shudder from the power of it, and then she sighed, and sagged against the carpet, spent.

After a moment he withdrew from her and rested next to her for a few minutes, his arm holding her close to his side. And then as the fire burned low, he scooped her into his arms, and carried her to the massive bed where he slid her between soft white sheets.

"Sleep," he said, smoothing her hair back from her face and kissing her forehead and then her nose and finally her lips. "You need your rest."

She murmured agreement, snuggling into the

impossibly soft pillow and smooth, cool sheets that felt so good against her heated skin. "Will you sleep, too?" she whispered.

"Yes."

An hour later, Zale lay on his back in bed listening to Emmeline's soft even breathing. He'd told her he would sleep. He wished he could sleep. Instead his mind raced.

Making love to Emmeline tonight changed everything. They were committed now. As good as married.

He'd thought he'd be uncertain, or regretful. He wasn't. He was glad Emmeline was his.

But this hadn't just been sex. It'd been more like...love. He hadn't planned on love. He was only now starting to like her. Love was not part of the deal.

The fact that he felt so much made him just want her that much more.

In the past, sex was like exercise—a great workout and a welcome release, giving him a good night's sleep.

But tonight he couldn't sleep. Instead he was lying awake, seething with chaotic emotions, new emotions, intense emotions.

He did not want the emotions. He did not want

anything to do with feelings, especially if they could trip him up, cloud his thinking.

He desired Emmeline, wanted Emmeline, would soon marry Emmeline, but he didn't know how she felt about him.

Yes, she desired him. After all, tonight she'd been hot, wet, astonishingly responsive. He'd made her come tonight—twice—but could there be more between them? Could there be love?

Tonight kissing her, buried deep in her, he'd felt lost in her, felt lost in something he'd forgotten even existed. Light. Warmth. Joy.

She felt like something you waited for…something special, magical…like the feeling you got as a child on Christmas morning.

Baffled by the dark tangle of his emotions, Zale rolled onto his side to look down at her, her elegant profile barely visible in the dark.

He'd known for years she was to be his. He'd known since he was fifteen she was the one chosen for him. But he'd never expected this…never expected this overwhelming desire to keep her, protect her, not just now, but forever.

CHAPTER NINE

HANNAH woke up early the next morning in a very dark room, in a strange bed, feeling utterly disoriented. And then turning over, she bumped against a very large, warm, solid person and it all came back to her.

She was in Zale's room, in his bed, naked.

Bits and pieces of the past night came to her. Guilt pummeled her. Why had she let this happen? How could she have let it happen?

Worse, how could she have enjoyed it so much?

But it had been amazing. *He'd* been amazing and last night he'd managed with his talented hands and mouth and body to sweep away her better judgment, as well as any inhibitions…

Blushing in the dark, she remembered how she'd practically screamed his name as she came…so really, truly mortifying. Hannah couldn't imagine Emmeline screaming during sex. Couldn't imagine that a proper princess would lose control like that…

Hannah rolled back over onto her stomach and

pressed her face into her pillow, and let out a muffled shout.

"I can hear that," Zale said dryly, next to her in the dark. "Anything you'd care to share?"

She pushed up onto her elbows and looked his way although the heavy drapes and blackout shades made it impossible to see. "I threw myself at you."

"I liked it," he said, shifting onto his own back and plumping pillows behind his head. "You did, too."

"I know I did, but…" she gritted, throwing back the covers and about to leave the bed when Zale's hand shot out, caught her by the wrist and pulled her toward him.

"But what?" he demanded, rising over her, straddling her hips and pinning her arms down over her head.

The air against her bare breasts made her nipples tighten and goose bumps danced across her skin. She arched against the pressure of his hands, which just made her nipples pebble harder.

She felt Zale shift, his hips sinking against her as his head dipped, his lips claiming one of her taut nipples, taking it into his warm, damp mouth.

Hannah shivered as he sucked on the sensitive bud, his tongue lazily flicking and then stroking until her hips strained up, pushing against him.

His body was hard, his shaft long and rigid, the thick, rounded head pushing at the juncture of her thighs. All she had to do was bend her knees, open her legs…

And then she did, sliding her legs open beneath the weight of his, allowing his body to settle lower, the head of his shaft teasing her inner lips, nudging her hot, slick opening.

She wiggled beneath him, needing more but he didn't push forward, didn't do anything other than lift his head and move to the other breast, giving the tender nipple the same attention he'd shown the first.

Hannah panted and wiggled again, lifting her hips up to grind against him. The smooth silken head of his shaft rubbed up and down her opening, sliding over her clitoris and then down over her wetness. She shivered and trembled and wiggled again.

He sucked harder on her nipple and she nearly screamed out loud. "Zale," she choked, skin hot, and unbearably sensitive. "Fill me."

He didn't need a second invitation. Using his knees he parted her thighs wider, and pushed against her entrance, stretching her open and sinking deeply into her body, which was definitely hot, wet, ready.

Last night the tempo had been slow, leisurely, but he took her hard now, driving into her as if he was trying to prove a point, teach her a lesson. But Hannah loved the sensation and friction, welcomed his hardness and heat and the way he filled her, making her forget everything but him.

There was just him. Him and her. Him with her. Him forever with her.

She was going to come again but the sensation of it was almost too much. She felt too much, felt pleasure and love.

Felt love.

Not possible, couldn't be, but that's what she felt. She loved him. Loved him completely.

She closed her eyes at the dizzying rush of white-hot sensation, the pleasure so sharp it was excruciating. She pressed her feet into the mattress and dug her fingers into his shoulders, skin pressed to skin as her control slipped and the orgasm took her.

"Emmeline." Zale ground out her name, loud, hoarse, his powerful body tensing, muscles clenching, as his body emptied into hers.

Emmeline.

Hannah slowly opened her eyes, aware of the warm weight of Zale on her, and the strength of his thighs between hers, and his thick erection still hot inside her body.

Emmeline.

Oh, God. This entire time, it hadn't been them, not him and her, but him and Emmeline.

Because that's who he wanted, Emmeline. Not Hannah, never Hannah. Hannah was nothing and nobody.

Her eyes burned. Hot. Scalding. She tried to blink but couldn't, frozen, shattered, stuck.

Stuck in a part she'd created, stuck in a lie she'd perpetuated.

If Zale found out the truth, he'd hate her. He'd never forgive her.

And did she blame him? She'd done everything he despised most—tricked, manipulated and played him.

Zale's hand touched her cheek, catching a tear as it fell. "Emmeline, why are you crying?"

"I'm not."

He gently touched the tip of his finger with the tear to her lips. "Trust me. You can tell me. You can tell me anything."

Trust me...you can tell me anything...

Her chest squeezed so tight her heart felt as if it would burst. "Everything's good," she said, fighting to keep her voice from breaking.

"Then why the tears?"

"Happy," she choked out, gulping air as fresh hot tears welled. "Just happy to be with you."

Hannah squeezed her eyes shut as Zale settled onto his side and drew her close, exhaling in a sigh of utter satisfaction.

He sounded relaxed, sated, happy, while she writhed inwardly, tormented by self-loathing.

She was bad, bad, bad…so bad. What had she done? How could she have done it?

Horrified and ashamed that she'd sleep with Emmeline's fiancé, Hannah pressed the soft sheets to her chest, regret filling her, making her conscience hurt and heart sting.

She should have told him the truth yesterday. Should have confessed her part in the charade, accepted the consequences and then gone home.

Or at the very least, she should have just gone home.

Instead she'd stayed, allowing herself to be seduced by her senses, and this impossible fantasy. As if she could be a princess. As if her life was a fairy tale.

Worse, she hadn't stayed for Emmeline. She'd stayed for herself. Stayed for the most selfish of reasons—she'd wanted Zale. And so she'd taken what wasn't hers.

And now the reality of her foolishness, and self-ishness, was hitting her like a sledgehammer.

Zale stroked her hip, a slow, lazy caress. "We didn't get a lot of sleep last night and yet we both have busy days."

"Do we?"

"I've meetings this morning, and you need to finish sitting for your portrait. Once done with that, I'll have Krek give you a tour of our private wing and then hopefully we can meet for lunch."

"You don't have to worry about me. I don't need entertaining," she said, trying to ignore the warmth of his hand as it moved leisurely up and down her body making her feel cherished and beautiful. "I've got plenty to do."

"I'm sure you do, but you said that you wanted to learn everything you could about me so I've arranged for Krek to take you on a tour."

"I won't be adding to his workload, will I?"

"No. Krek lives for this sort of thing," he answered, kissing her cheek before pulling away. He left the bed and crossed to the window, to pull back the heavy drapes, allowing the morning light to flood the room.

Hannah blinked at the light, and rubbed her eyes before pushing a tumble of heavy hair back from her face.

Zale was still standing at the window, gazing out over the walled city to the sea. He was naked and completely comfortable with it. But of course he would be. He had that sinfully sexy body—big shoulders, rock hard stomach, a small, firm butt and those long, lean muscular legs.

He was so perfect. She was not. "Can I have my coat please?" she asked, sitting up and still holding the sheet to her breasts.

"I can't believe you're shy," he said, collecting her nightgown and coat and carrying it to her. "I've heard you sunbathe topless on friends' yachts."

Hannah wrinkled her nose, unable to imagine going topless in public.

But then, her father had been very strict when Hannah was growing up. He'd frequently reminded her that her mother had been a lady and Hannah would be a lady, too. Which meant no short shorts or revealing tops. She hadn't been allowed to date until she was sixteen and even then it had to be on a group date. Anyone she wanted to date had to come to the ranch and be grilled for an hour by her dad, so mostly, no boys in Bandera wanted to.

"It's chilly," she said, taking the coat from him and sliding one arm into a sleeve, and then the other before knotting the sash tightly about her waist.

Head held high, Hannah rose from the bed, prepared to dash out of the bedroom, but Zale caught her by the wrist as she passed, pulling her toward him.

"You keep surprising me," he said hoarsely, holding her against him. The coat provided little protection. She could feel the entire length of him, from his thick chest to his warm torso and firm, narrow hips.

She sucked in a breath, heat surging to her cheeks as his body hardened against her. "Is that good or bad?"

The expression in his eyes was possessive. "Both." He drew his thumb across her mouth, his gaze fixed to her soft lips as they parted in a silent gasp.

"How can it be both good and bad?" she whispered, licking her dry lips.

"You're more than I expected." He hesitated. "Which is good."

"So what is bad?"

He slowly dragged his thumb across her bottom lip, tugging it down, making her feel alarmingly exposed. "How much I want you. *Still.*"

His words and touch were unbearably erotic. She shuddered in response, her defenses caving. He made her feel so carnal. Made her want all the things that were forbidden.

Like him.

"I've just had you, three times in the past nine hours. I shouldn't need you again," he added, his voice deepening, rougher than usual, even as his shaft rose against her belly, an insistent nudge that made her feel weak. Every time he touched her, she melted. Just one touch and she became his.

His, she repeated silently, dazed by the waves of pleasure surging through her one after the other. He made her feel drunk but it was on passion and emotion.

She'd never felt anything close to this with anyone, and she didn't think she'd ever feel this way about anyone else, either.

"And that's bad?" she asked unsteadily.

He tugged the coat back from her shoulder, exposing one full pale breast.

"Yes." He cupped her breast and she exhaled at the warmth of his hand against her cool skin. He stroked the soft underside, a light teasing caress that made her nerve endings dance and her lower back tingle.

"But you don't really need me," she whispered, trying her best to stay coherent—rational, knowing she needed to focus. But thinking was virtually impossible when she was so overwhelmed by sensation. "You've had plenty—"

"But apparently not plenty enough," he contradicted, as his erection grew bigger, thicker.

She rubbed against him, feeling the broad rounded tip, remembering how amazing it had felt last night as he entered her, slowly, deeply.

The memory made her shudder and he groaned as she rubbed against him.

With a muttered oath he caught her hips in his hands, pressed her even more firmly to him, his breathing ragged. "I don't want to want you this much."

"I don't want to want you this much, either," she flung breathlessly at him, as his hand moved down to cup her backside. He was kneading her cheek, squeezing and lifting the cheek away from the other, as if to part her legs and make room for him between.

The sensation of his hands on her butt, the feeling of being opened for him, was so provocative her legs nearly gave away.

"Yes, you do," he answered, lowering his head to kiss her, his lips and teeth nipping at her lips. "You are so hot you're almost on fire."

It was true. Little stars exploded in her head and Hannah pressed her thighs tight, sending rivulets of pleasure everywhere. She wasn't just hot, she was wet, and desperate for him to fill her, answering the terrible ache throbbing inside of her. "You're deliberately turning me on, making it impossible to function—"

He cut her off with a kiss, the pressure of his mouth parting her lips, his tongue taking her mouth as if it belonged to him. She loved the way he kissed her—hard, fierce—and she wrapped her arms around his neck, holding him closer. With his cool tongue in her mouth and his hands against her heated skin she thought she'd let him do anything, have anything.

The handsome clock on the gold marble mantel suddenly chimed, and continued to chime repeatedly.

Zale lifted his head, listened to the chiming of the clock. "Can't be," he muttered, glancing at his watch then pushing her firmly away. "This is what I mean. I have a meeting in just a few minutes and yet I am still here."

"Not my fault!"

"No, I know. It's mine." His gaze swept over her. "But that's the part I don't like. Because self-control has never been a problem. Not until I met you." Then with a short, sharp shake of his head, he walked into his adjoining bath to shower, shave and start his day.

Dazed, body numb, Hannah climbed back into bed and drew the covers up to her chin.

She was lost. And she wanted her own life back. She needed it, and she needed to be herself. And Zale needed to know the truth.

She had to tell him.

Had to let him know she wasn't his Emmeline.

Hannah must have fallen asleep because the next thing she heard was the sound of Celine wheeling a breakfast trolley laden with tempting treats into her room.

Celine positioned the trolley next to the bed and began uncovering dishes—strawberries and cream, buttery croissants, warm savory meat pastries, poached eggs, Greek yogurt, granola, fresh squeezed orange juice and a tall silver pot of coffee.

"His Majesty thought you might enjoy breakfast in bed today," Celine said, transforming the trolley into a table next to the bed, acting as if it was perfectly normal for Hannah to be in the king's bed.

Hannah sat up. "All for me?"

"His Majesty said you've a long day of appointments, activities and meetings, starting with this morning's portrait sitting, so you'll need a good breakfast. And once you've eaten, we'll return to the Queen's Chambers and get you ready for your portrait sitting."

Emmeline's personal stylists were waiting for her as she emerged from her bathroom a half hour later, swaddled in a Turkish towel.

Camille had everything ready to do Hannah's hair and it wasn't long before Hannah was back in the dress she was wearing for her portrait, the pale shimmering gown clinging to her curves, the color highlighting her golden beauty, as Camille ran the flat iron over the ends of her hair making sure it was perfectly straight.

Teresa was passing time by sitting on a stool and flipping through a magazine, sometimes reading an article aloud. Suddenly she stopped flipping pages to stare at a photograph.

"There she is!" Teresa exclaimed. "That Hannah Smith, Your Highness, the American lookalike we told you about in Palm Beach."

"The one you said helped organize the polo tournament?" Hannah answered vaguely.

Camille smoothed a strand of hair with the flat iron. "Yes, and it's a shame you didn't meet her. Teresa and I were dying to see the two of you to-gether…would have been fascinating."

"Mmm." Hannah feigned boredom. "You said she's in the magazine?"

"Yes. This week's issue." Teresa drew the magazine closer to study the photo and caption. "They snapped her leaving a South Beach nightclub and she's with someone who isn't happy at all…oooh! Sheikh Makin Al-Koury. It looks like he's dragging her out of the club." Teresa glanced up at Hannah. "I wonder if that's her boyfriend?"

Hannah's brows flattened. "I thought she just worked for him?"

"I don't know, but he looks really ticked off. He's practically dragging her out of the club." Teresa grinned. "Just like a jealous boyfriend."

"What does the caption say?"

"Not much, just *Sheikh Al-Koury and unidentified friend leaving Lounge Mynt.*" Teresa looked up. "Although that is a really trendy club. Impossible to get into unless you're a VIP."

"I'm sure they're not dating," Hannah said firmly, staggered by the news that Emmeline and Makin Al-Koury were together. "Sheikhs do not date their secretaries." Hannah impatiently held her hand out for the magazine. "Can I see?"

Teresa slid off the stool and carried the magazine to Hannah. "There," she said, holding the magazine out to Hannah while Camille peeked over her shoulder for a look, too. "Doesn't he look angry with her?"

Hannah couldn't believe her eyes. It *was* Emmeline and Makin stepping out of a South Beach nightclub, which was all the more incredible because Sheikh Makin Al-Koury did not go to nightclubs, avoiding places celebs and paparazzi hung out. He was a very private man and never dated women who liked the limelight.

She glanced from Makin Al-Koury to Emmeline. Emmeline looked terrible. Gaunt. Frail. Eyes deeply shadowed. "She doesn't look well," Hannah said. "She's too thin."

Camille leaned closer to the photo. "She's probably partying too much. Everyone does everything in South Beach."

"Not Makin," Hannah said under her breath, thinking Teresa was right. Makin looked absolutely livid in the photo. What was going on between them? What were they doing together? And when had Princess Emmeline met up with Hannah's boss?

"What's everyone looking at?" Zale asked from the doorway.

Hannah jumped and shoved the magazine back into Teresa's hands. "Nothing."

"Nothing?" he drawled, entering the dressing room. "Then why do all three of you look guilty?"

"Because we were all drooling over clothes. Expensive clothes. Something you'd never do," Hannah answered with a laugh. "What brings you here, Your Majesty?"

"You."

His rich voice and Raguvian accent made everything he said sound sinful. Sexy.

Heat swept through her. Her cheeks burned as she turned in her chair to face him. He was wearing a dress shirt and dark slacks and yet he looked incredibly fit, as though he'd just returned from a long run. "I'm honored."

"How are the preparations coming for your sitting?"

"Good. Just need my makeup and I'm off."

Camille and Teresa discreetly disappeared and Zale approached her carrying a large black velvet box.

"I have a gift," he said. "Something I should have given you when you first arrived."

She tipped her head back, looked him straight in the eyes, loving the heat in his amber gaze. "But you haven't been sure about me."

"That's true." He handed the velvet box to her. "But I'm sure now."

Hannah opened the lid of the black box, revealing a tall, glittering tiara.

"It was my mother's," he said, "and my grandmother's before that."

It was stunning, beyond stunning, the delicate diamond arch sparkling, catching the light, reflecting it in every direction. It was classic and simple and breathtaking. "I can't possibly accept this," she whispered, "it's far too valuable. It's a family heirloom—"

"Of course you can. It's mine to give," he interrupted. "And I give it to you, just the first of many, Emmeline. Once you become my queen, you will be showered in jewels."

The possessive light in his eyes made her breath catch. "You really intend to marry me?"

"Yes."

"No doubts?"

"No. Once I made love to you, I committed myself. We're as good as married. There's no turning back."

CHAPTER TEN

HANNAH tried not to panic.

Zale said there was no turning back. They were as good as married. Which would be a huge problem if Emmeline failed to show up.

Emmeline had to show up.

What would Hannah do?

The wedding was a week away. The world expected a magnificent royal wedding, a wedding that was to be televised to the world. Emmeline couldn't just bail on Zale at the last minute. It wouldn't be right. Wasn't fair. To string him along throughout their engagement and then to fail to show for the wedding...

Hannah needed to tell him the truth. But how would she tell him? How to break the news?

Hey, King Patek, I'm not actually your betrothed, but Hannah Smith from Bandera, Texas, and I am here to keep you occupied while your real fiancée sorts some things out in Palm Beach.

Sick at heart, stomach churning like mad, Hannah

pressed her hands together, and tried to push the anxious thoughts out of her mind. Emmeline would come. Emmeline had said she'd come. Emmeline wouldn't break her word.

A half hour later Celine helped Hannah change from the elegant evening gown into a pretty navy silk skirt and white blouse for Hannah's palace tour with Krek. She wore fat pearls at her throat, a pearl and diamond bracelet on her wrist and medium-heel shoes that would be comfortable to walk in.

"As you know, I am one of the most senior staff members," Krek said, meeting her in the sitting room of the Queen's Chambers. "I have served the Patek family for nearly thirty-five years now, starting as a footman to the late queen, before becoming butler for His Majesty. As head butler at the Patek Palace, I am responsible for all private and official entertaining both here and abroad. I organize and attend state banquets and receptions, ensuring that every detail is properly, professionally and elegantly handled."

"That's a great deal of responsibility," Hannah answered.

"It is, Your Highness, but this is what I've done my whole life. I can't imagine doing anything else."

They'd walked down the large corridor, descended the stairs and he opened the doors to a gorgeous light-filled room painted a vivid yellow contrasted by ornate white moldings.

"This was Queen Madeleine's favorite room," he said, leading her inside. The high ceiling of the room was painted sky-blue with white billowy clouds. "Yellow was Queen Madeleine's favorite color as it reminded her of the sun and this was where she preferred to entertain." He glanced at her. "Did you ever meet her? She was your grandmother's first cousin."

Hannah's mouth opened and shut. "I...I don't recall."

"You would if you had met her. She was a lovely woman. We had quite a good relationship and I was very happy working for her, but when Princess Helena—His Majesty's mother—arrived from Greece to marry His Majesty's father, King Stephen IV, I was assigned to the newlyweds' household."

"Did you mind the switch?"

"Not at all. King Stephen and Princess Helena were a delight to work for. They, too, were an arranged marriage but soon after the wedding fell in love."

"They had a happy marriage then?"

"The happiest." It was Zale who'd answered and Hannah inhaled sharply, his deep voice sinfully sexy. Zale had entered through a side door and he walked toward them now.

"The two of them were inseparable through thick and thin, and they certainly had their fair share of challenges."

"Your Majesty," Krek said with a formal bow as Zale joined them. "We haven't made it very far yet."

"Perhaps I can take over?" Zale suggested.

Krek bowed again. "Of course, Your Majesty." He tipped his head in Hannah's direction. "Your Highness." And then he was gone, quietly, discreetly.

"Enjoying the tour?" Zale asked.

"Yes," she answered. "But we really only just started."

"Then let's continue," he answered, leading her to the adjoining room, the Crimson Room, which had been the favorite reception room for Zale's grandfather, King Stephen Mikal. "In this room my grandfather, King Mikal, entertained the Tsar, a Sultan, two British kings, a dozen dukes, as well as a Pope."

"Did you ever know him?"

"He died when I was fourteen months old, but apparently he spent a lot of time with Stephen and me. We have quite a few photos of us together."

"Were you and Prince Stephen close growing up?"

"Yes. But that didn't mean we always got along. We could be quite competitive." Zale's expression was rueful. "At least, I was."

"You fought?"

"Fistfights? No. But every now and then we'd challenge each other to a race or a wrestling match and then it was a battle to end all battles." Zale smiled. "Mind you, Stephen was two and a half years older than me, and I was scrawny until my midteens, but there was no way I'd let Stephen take me without a fight."

Hannah couldn't imagine Zale small. "Define scrawny."

"Skinny, lanky, short."

"I can't believe it."

"Neither could I. I hated it. But at least I had speed."

Her pulse quickened. Zale appealed to her at every level. "So when did you grow? Because no one could call you scrawny now."

"I shot up nearly six inches when I was seventeen. Grew another four inches at eighteen. And kept growing until I turned twenty. But it's hard being taken seriously in football when you're so small. Fortunately it forced me to work hard, harder than everyone around me, and my work ethic was born."

"I admire your work ethic."

"It helped make me who I am."

Zale opened the doors to a bright, vast, high-ceiling hall lined with portraits. "We're now entering the Royal Gallery. All the portraits of Raguva's kings and queens hang here. Your portrait will join mine after it's completed—"

"We're really going to marry?"

"Yes. Sex sealed the deal, Emmeline. I told you it would. It's in the prenup, part of our contract. By making love, you became mine."

They were standing before a large portrait of a dark-haired, brown-eyed king that looked remarkably like Zale.

She shivered. His.

He reached out to tuck a pale blond tendril of hair behind her ear. "We can be happy."

She felt lost in his eyes. "You really think so?"

"Yes."

Her eyes burned and her throat ached and she had to turn away so he wouldn't see her cry. "How can you be so sure?"

"Because I have strong feelings for you."

His tone had been light, teasing and yet suddenly

her chest constricted, air bottled in her lungs. If she were good…

But she was not good. Nor was Emmeline. Because they were both duplicitous. Both betraying him.

"I think we've seen enough," he said. "Let's go to lunch. I have something special planned."

He led her downstairs, through a hall and then another, into an old wing of the palace that looked more like a castle than a palace.

"The original fortress," Zale said as soldiers before them opened a thick wooden door studded with metal that led to a narrow stairwell.

"This was the keep, built in the late fourteenth century and enlarged and strengthened in the 1500s," he said, taking her hand as they walked up the winding staircase, which was cool and dimly lit. "For hundreds of years kings have made new additions to the castle, and modernized existing wings, turning the fortress into something more palatial, but this part remains as it was five hundred years ago."

They climbed at least three floors until they reached the top of the tower and Zale pushed open another door, revealing blue sky and impossibly thick stone walls.

"The castle parapet," Zale said. "My favorite place growing up."

They were up high, in the tallest point of the castle and it was a gorgeous day with a blue sky and not a cloud in sight. The spring air was crisp and flags snapped below them in the wind, with the breeze carrying a hint of salt from the sea.

"I can see why you like it here," she said, joining him at the thick wall and leaning against the weathered stone warmed from the sun. "A place a boy can escape to, and where a king can think."

"That's exactly it." Zale leaned on the wall, too, his shoulders flexed, his weight resting on his forearms. "Here I have quiet and space. Perspective. I find perspective is essential. Far too easy sometimes to get caught up in emotions or the stress of a situation, whether real or imagined."

She would have never guessed he could get caught up in emotions. He seemed far too level-headed for that. "Thank you for bringing me here."

"We're not done yet." He extended his hand to her. "Come. Let's eat."

But instead of leading her back down the stairs, they continued walking around the parapet to the other side where a round tower was in ruins, with just pieces of walls and without a roof. The stairwell had been cemented over and a new stone floor mortared into place.

In the center of the ruined tower was a small round table with two chairs. The table was covered in a pale rose linen cloth with a loose floral arrangement of roses, freesias and lilies in the middle. There were two place settings, with sterling cutlery, gold-rimmed china topped with silver covers and tall, delicate stemware adding sparkle to the table.

"Your Royal Highness," Zale said, drawing a chair out from the round table for her. "If you'd please."

"Thank you."

He helped scoot her chair in, the legs scraping against the stone. "I enjoyed our picnic on the beach so much I thought we should have another meal where it was just you and me. I rather like not having staff waiting on us. It's more relaxed."

"And more fun," she added, thinking that while she'd enjoyed the picnic on his island, this was the most gorgeous, romantic setting she could imagine. "Thank you."

"It's my pleasure," he answered, sitting opposite her and drawing a bottle of white wine from an impressive silver bucket where it'd been chilling. He opened the bottle and filled each of their goblets. "To you, to me, and our future together," he said, his gaze holding hers and lifting his glass in a toast.

Her eyes burned hotter and she had to smile to keep the tears back. "To our future," she echoed, clinking the rim of her glass to his.

He searched her eyes, looking for something, but what, she didn't know.

"Cheers," he said.

They clinked glasses again and then drank and Hannah had never been so grateful for the warmth of the wine as it slipped down her throat and heated her stomach. She was cold on the inside, cold and scared.

This was going to end badly. So badly.

And then to cover the almost unbearable pain, she leaned forward to smell one of the sweetly scented roses. "They smell like real roses. Thank goodness."

He looked at her, mildly amused. "When did roses stop smelling like roses?"

"A number of years back when someone got the idea to make them more hardy and disease resistant. The flowers grew bigger but the fragrance disappeared."

"I didn't know that."

"I don't suppose there's a section on rose horti-culture in your how-to-be-a-king manual."

"Regrettably there isn't such a manual. I could have used one."

"Why?"

"The first few years were hard. Every day I wished I'd spent time with my father learning about my responsibilities before he died. There's so much he could have taught me, so much I needed to know."

"But that would have meant giving up your career sooner."

"I know. I wasn't ready to give up football. I probably would never have been ready. But then they died and their accident forced me to grow up."

She was silent a moment. "Is that how you really view it?"

"I was the Crown Prince. I should have been here, learning from my father."

"But football was your passion. You loved it since you were a boy."

His broad shoulders shifted. "Boys become men."

She reached out, covered his hand with hers. "It's none of my business, but I'm glad you were able to do what you loved to do. So many people are miserable. They hate their jobs, hate their lives. It's not the way I want to live."

"You're happy then?"

"I love my work. I'm lucky I get to do what I do."

He smiled at her then and his smile transformed his face from handsome to absolutely gorgeous.

If only she could tell him the truth. She needed him to know.

Her eyes burned and she took a quick sip of her wine to hide her pain.

Zale reached out and brushed a long pale strand of hair back from her cheek. "You keep tearing up today. What's wrong? What have I done?"

"Nothing. I'm just thinking about the past and the future and our families."

"There's been a lot of pressure from our families, hasn't there?"

She nodded.

"You know my father was the one that wanted us to marry. He picked you for me when I was fifteen." His lips twisted. "You were five. And chubby. I was horrified."

Hannah smiled crookedly. "I would have been horrified, too."

"My father assured me that you'd grow up, and once you did, you'd be a rare beauty. He was right. You…fit me."

"I'm glad."

"Are you?"

"Very much so."

"So no regrets about last night?"

"None at all. I love—" She broke off, aware that she'd come so close to telling him how she felt. Because she did. "I loved every moment of it."

"We should probably get the prenup signed. Your father calls me every day, sometimes twice a day, to ask why we haven't done it yet."

"And what do you tell him?"

"That we'll sign it when we're ready."

"I can't imagine he likes that."

"No. But this is between you and me now, and I intend to keep it that way."

"Do we need the prenup then? Can't we just get married without it?"

Zale studied her from across the table. "You'd marry me without any financial agreement in place?"

"I trust you."

"You should. I'd never betray you."

Guilt flooded her. Guilt and grief.

But even as she battled her conscience, she told herself to remember it all.

Every word.

Every smile.

Every detail.

She wanted to remember it all so that even when

she was gone she'd have at least the memories to hold, memories of lunch with Zale in the crumbling tower overlooking the walled city nestled between mountains and sea.

Because this wasn't just the day she fell in love, but the day she fell in love with him forever.

Less than a week ago she knew practically nothing about Raguva, Zale's small independent country overlooking the sapphire Adriatic Sea, and even less about him, Zale Ilia Patek, Raguva's king, but now Hannah knew far too much.

Like how driven Zale Patek was, and how determined he could be.

How his country meant so much to him and his brother even more so.

It'd break her heart to leave. And she would leave. If not tonight, then tomorrow. It wasn't a maybe, it was definite. Simply a matter of time.

A question of when.

"Would you have been attracted to me if we'd met a different way?" she asked.

He seemed intrigued by her question. "You mean, if we'd just met randomly…two people on the street?"

She nodded.

His brow lowered and he studied her so intently

that she felt as though he could see all the way through. "Yes. Definitely."

If anyone else had looked at her so closely it would have made her uncomfortable, but when Zale looked at her like this she felt beautiful…safe.

Yes, safe. He was a warrior. A protector. A man with courage and integrity.

"Would you like me?" he asked, leaning back in his chair.

Her eyes stung.

Absolutely. Most definitely. "Yes."

His lips curved, and his amber gaze warmed. "So the prince and princess rode off into the sunset and lived happily ever after?"

The lump in her throat was making it hard to breathe. "I hope so."

"Me, too." Still smiling, he looked down at the silver dome covering his plate. "And maybe while we're in agreement, should we eat?"

She nodded and lifted the silver cover off her plate revealing a cold seafood salad with a small plate of fresh rolls and sweet butter. "Looks delicious," she said, knowing she wouldn't be able to swallow more than a mouthful.

"Yes," he agreed, looking at her instead of his plate. "Absolutely delicious."

She blushed, her body coming alive, lower back

tingling, breasts aching. "How can I possibly eat now?"

"Maybe we just skip lunch and head back to my room—"

"No!" she cut him off with a breathless laugh. "Absolutely not."

"Absolutely not? Was last night that bad?"

She choked on a muffled laugh, even as bitter-sweet emotion filled her, flooding her, reminding her to again remember everything…his expression, his strong features, the sensual curve of his lip, the searing heat in his eyes.

Remember, she told herself, remember his warmth and the smell of his cologne and the way he smiles when he looks at you and likes what he sees…

Like now.

"You know it was great."

"Thank God. I was beginning to worry there."

She smothered another laugh, loving him like this…lighthearted, teasing, entertaining. "I just wanted to stay because it's so beautiful here and you went to so much trouble arranging this lunch. But if you want to go, we can."

"You're letting me make the decision?"

She made a face. "You are the king."

His warm gaze moved slowly across her face,

lingering on her full lips. "We'll stay," he said at length. "We'll eat. But as soon as we're done, I'm taking you to my bed."

CHAPTER ELEVEN

Hannah struggled to chew her food but it was nearly impossible with all the butterflies flitting inside her belly. Zale didn't help matters by giving her that I'm-so-hungry-I-could-eat-you look throughout the meal.

After a half dozen bites she gave up and sipped her wine, drinking one glass, and then another. By the time she'd finished the second glass, she knew she'd drunk too much.

Not because she was drunk. But because she was a little too hot, a little too turned on. Already.

"You're not eating," Zale said, noticing her plate was virtually untouched and his was nearly empty. "Didn't care for the lobster? It's one of my favorites."

"I do. It was good."

"How would you know? You ate nothing."

She took a quick breath, cheeks warm, limbs unusually heavy. Even her pulse felt slow. "I'm happy, though."

"Are you?"

"I'll never forget it. The view. The flowers. The conversation with you."

He smiled, amused. "That's a lot to remember."

"I know, but it's worth it. How many women get to do something like this? Lunch with King Zale Patek in one of his parapet towers overlooking the sea? Not many."

"No. Just you."

Something in his eyes made her heart jump. He was looking at her as if she mattered.

"We'll have to do it again one day," he promised, that faint smile playing at his lips while his amber eyes held hers. "Maybe on our first anniversary."

"I'd like that," she whispered, knowing that she wouldn't be the one here, that she'd never have any of this again but she wouldn't think about leaving, not now, not when she had the rest of the day, the night and possibly tomorrow.

"There's something else I'd like, Your Majesty," she said, voice barely audible.

"And what is that, Your Highness?"

For a moment Hannah couldn't speak, not when her throat squeezed closed and her heart felt as if it were being torn to pieces. And then she pressed the intense emotions back, refusing to let pain steal a single minute of what was left of the day. "I'd like you to kiss me."

Heat burned in his eyes. His nostrils flared. Hannah could practically feel his desire.

He left his chair, pulled her from her seat and pressed her back against one of the remaining walls. He leaned close, crowding her, his chest against her breasts, his lean hips teasing hers. He was lean, hard, hot and dropping his head he brushed his lips across hers in a kiss so soft and light that she groaned deep in her throat.

"How's that?" he murmured, his lips pressing a kiss to the hollow beneath her ear. "Was that good?"

"No."

"No? Why not?"

His breath was warm on the cool curve of her ear and made her tingle with pleasure. "Not enough," she murmured, sliding her hands up the broad planes of his chest. His chest was hard, thickly muscled, and she ran her hands over the firm, dense muscle.

"Want more," she said. "Want you to kiss me properly."

"Like this?" he asked, nibbling at her earlobe.

She felt the coiling of desire in her belly and the dampness between her thighs. Her womb actually ached, her innermost places empty, wanting him. "No. A real kiss. A proper kiss to make the day perfect."

"You've already made it perfect," he said, catching her face in his hand, and lifting her chin up to look down into her eyes before capturing her mouth with his.

He kissed her slowly, gently, coaxing a response from her, at first warm and sweet, and then warm and sweet became desperate and hot. His lips parted hers and his tongue took her mouth and Hannah wound her arms up around his neck, unable to get close enough.

She needed him, wanted him, wanted everything with him—marriage, and babies, and growing old together—but she wouldn't have that, she'd only have this.

And she'd take this, all of this, and somehow she'd make it be enough.

She could feel the stubble on his jaw, smell that subtle cologne he wore, taste the wine on his tongue.

"Need you," she murmured against his mouth, as she slipped her fingers into the short crisp hair at his nape. "Need you so much..."

He broke off the kiss, lifting his head to look down at her. His chest rose and fell with deep breaths and his eyes were cloudy with desire and she reached up to touch his mouth with her fingertips, awed by everything she felt for him.

It was magnificent.

And terrifying.

"You are so damn beautiful," he said, pressing a kiss to her fingertips. "I honestly can't get enough of you."

"Then don't."

Jaw thick, eyes narrowed, he lifted her into his arms, carried her to a broken stone in the shadows of the turret and set her on the edge. Pushing back her skirt he exposed her bare legs and parted her pale thighs to reveal the scrap of thong she wore. "Unbelievably hot," he growled, lightly running a fingertip over the damp silk thong between her thighs, making the fabric even wetter.

She gasped as his finger traced her swollen lips again and again, making her thighs quiver and her insides clench with need.

"So wet," he muttered, fascinated by the bit of silk outlining her most intimate places, and stroking it even more slowly to feel her shudder against his hand.

"And so eager for more," he added, voice rough, raspy, before pulling the scrap of silk away from her body. He swore beneath his breath as he caught sight of her inner lips and her pink, glistening core.

Hannah clutched the sides of the broken stone she sat on, unable to breathe. No man had looked at her so closely, so intently and she tried to close her thighs but Zale was crouching between, his thighs holding hers open.

"What is it about you?" he groaned, lightly sliding his fingers up and down the wet tender flesh. "Why do you do this to me?"

She jumped and cried out as his fingertips brushed against her, the nub already so sensitive she thought she might explode. "It's not…me…" she panted, fire licking her skin, making her burn, ache. "It's…you."

"No. I've never needed or wanted a woman the way I want you."

She gripped the stone even harder as he focused his attention on her, teasing the small nub, using the pad of his thumb to draw small light circles against the slick ridge.

Hannah could feel the pressure building within her, the coil of desire growing hotter, tighter, fiercer. She was close to climaxing but was too aware that Zale watched her face as he touched her, reading her emotions and reactions. It was sexy and yet scary—to be so open in front of a man—physically and emotionally.

There was so much at risk, she thought, struggling to breathe, already too dizzy. If she wasn't comfortable he'd see just how much she wanted him to take her, own her, make her forever his.

"Come," he said, "I want to watch you come."

She shook her head even as her body jerked and jumped, nerve endings stretched to breaking. "Can't," she choked, skin hot, body burning, desperate to find release but unable to let go when he'd watch her fall apart. She'd never been wild, never sexually adventurous, her college boyfriend going so far as to complain that she was boring in bed, but with Zale she felt positively daring.

Desperate.

Wanton.

"Yes, you can," he insisted.

"N-n-noooo. I c-c-c-can't," she stuttered, unable to meet his gaze even as her thighs trembled with the building pressure.

"Why not?" he murmured, gaze intent on her flushed face.

"You're…watching."

"I like watching. It gives me pleasure."

She shook her head, her lower lip caught between

her teeth. The tension within her was overwhelming. She couldn't hang on much longer.

"Then close your eyes."

She shook her head again and with a growl he parted her knees wider, and leaned in to cover her clitoris with his mouth. He sucked hard and when she bucked against him, he slid a finger into her, a slow upward thrust that hit a certain spot at the exact moment he suckled the nub.

She screamed, the sound wrenched from her as he shattered her control with an orgasm so intense her hips lifted off the stone.

But he didn't stop.

He kept sucking and thrusting a finger into her, deeper, steadily, rubbing against that magic invisible spot making her feel hot and tingly all over again. She wanted to tell him it'd never work, wanted to tell him she'd never come again but then he blew on her, a warm breath of air before slowly licking the taut ridge and sucking on the tiny tip.

She exploded a second time, screaming his name.

This time Hannah pushed him back with a shaking hand. "No more."

Still shuddering, she adjusted the wet thong over her swollen sensitive parts and pulled her skirt down over her legs.

"What did you do to me?" she choked out, her entire body rippling with aftershocks.

"What you do to me every time I look at you."

Hot salty tears stung her eyes and she wiped them away. "I think you broke me," she whispered, still shuddering and shaking.

He smiled crookedly and kissed her knee through her skirt and then higher on her thigh before standing.

She tipped her head back to look up at him. "What about you?" Her gaze dropped to his trousers and the fabric straining over his thick erection. "Don't you want anything?"

He looked at her for what felt like forever before extending his hand to her. "Yes. But in my room. Putting you on your hands and knees here won't be comfortable on the stone."

She gulped a breath. Hands and knees next? She'd never tried that yet. "Maybe we should."

Zale laughed softly and they made their way back across the parapet and down the circular staircase in the tower until they reached the ground floor.

They were on the way to the King's Chambers when one of the footmen stopped Zale and said that Mrs. Sivka needed him to help her with Prince Constantine.

Zale's jaw tightened, concern etched in his features. "I'll go directly," he told the footman, before turning to Hannah. "I'll find you in your room."

"Is there anything I can do?"

"Just wait for me."

She watched Zale walk with the footman toward Prince Constantine's suite, his stride long, quick. He was worried.

He's a good brother, she thought, an amazing man.

In her suite, she washed her hands and was still running a brush through her hair when she heard her phone vibrate in the nightstand drawer.

Emmeline!

Hannah raced to retrieve her phone. "Hello?"

"Hannah, it's me."

Hannah glanced behind her, making sure none of the staff members were nearby able to hear. "Are you okay?"

"I...I don't know."

"Are you coming?"

"I...don't...know."

Stunned, Hannah pressed a hand to her forehead, feeling as if she was close to losing her mind. "What do you mean, you don't know?"

"I'm in Kadar."

"Kadar? Sheikh Makin's country? Why?"

"He thinks I'm you."

"Tell him you're not!"

"I can't."

"Why not?"

"It'd ruin everything!"

Hannah darted another quick look over her shoulder and added more urgently. "But everything's already ruined! You have no idea what's happened—"

"I'm sorry, I am." Emmeline cut Hannah short, tears thickening her voice. "But everything's out of my control."

"*Your* control. *Your* life. It's always about *you,* isn't it?"

"I didn't mean it that way."

"But you did mean to send me here in your place and you didn't intend to come right away." Hannah was so angry she was practically shouting. "You used me. Manipulated me. But how do you think I feel being trapped here, pretending to—" She broke off as the floorboards creaked behind her.

She wasn't alone. Hannah spun around.

Zale.

She felt the blood drain from her face and for a moment there was just the roar in her ears and then nothing.

Silence and nothing.

She snapped the phone closed and it nearly slipped from her fingers.

"How is our good friend Alejandro?" Zale asked, taking a step into the room and closing her bedroom door behind him.

Hannah's heart thudded hard and she darted a panicked glance at the now closed door. "W-w-who?"

"Emmeline."

"It wasn't what you think."

"Of course you'd make it a game. Nothing is ever straightforward with you." He walked to the bed and sat down on the edge and then patted the mattress beside him. "So come, sit, we'll try to make this fun."

He smiled at her but his expression was cold. Angry. "Shall we play twenty questions? I'll ask, you answer—"

"Zale, it wasn't a man. It wasn't Alejandro. It was one of my girlfriends."

"And you expect me to believe that?"

"*Yes.*"

"I know what I heard. You were begging him to come get you and take you home."

"No! That wasn't it. I promise. Cross my heart—"

"Don't." His voice dropped, his tone pitched low and dangerous. "Don't do that."

Hannah crossed the carpet, shaking from head to toe. She thrust her phone out to him. "Call. Call the last number back. See who answers. It's not a man."

But he refused to take the phone and it fell between them, hitting the mattress and then sliding onto the floor next to the bed.

She'd never seen him this angry. He seethed with fury, amber eyes glittering like cut stone. After a moment he rose from the bed, circled her where she stood.

"Every time I get comfortable with you, you do this. Every time I commit to you, you play me for a fool."

"No." She laced her fingers together, skin prickling with unease. He was dangerous like this. Unpredictable. "I would never do that to you. Never." And then she heard herself and her vehemence and realized she *was* playing him for a fool. She had ever since she arrived.

Pretending to be Emmeline.

Pretending to be working out the differences in their relationship…

Pretending to get to know him before they married, when in reality, she wasn't even the one he'd ever marry…

"You're not a damsel in distress, Princess."

He spit the words out as if they hurt his mouth. "There's no lock on any door. No guard keeping you here. If you want to go. Go. As for me, I have things to do and I'm not going to stand here and waste another minute with you."

"Zale—"

He lifted a hand to silence her. "Enough. Have some respect. Please." Hand still lifted, he walked out the door.

CHAPTER TWELVE

ZALE left his room and returned to the old castle keep, crossing through the once grand medieval hall still lined with heraldic banners and suits of armor, to the new wing on the far side, a wing which he'd had built five years ago to house his personal gymnasium and sport facility.

The sport facility was really a world-class sport complex, containing a regulation football field on the first floor with real grass, nets and stadium lighting. The second floor was divided into various sport courts—one for tennis, basketball and handball—plus a weight room where he still trained every other day.

A locker room adjoined the weight room, outfitted with a sauna, a whirlpool and a massage table for rehabilitating injuries.

Not that Zale got injured anymore. But it made him feel connected to the person he'd been, the one who'd lived and breathed sport above everything. The sport facility hadn't been cheap, either. It'd cost him millions to build, but he'd used his own money and he maintained it with his own money, too. In this part of the palace he wasn't a king but a man. A man who needed nothing but a ball, a net, an expanse of grass.

In his locker room he stripped out of his dress shirt and trousers, changing into sweatpants, a T-shirt and his running shoes.

Today he wouldn't run on the treadmill. Today he ran on the track that circled his field, running fast, hard, one kilometer and then another and another but no matter how fast he ran he couldn't escape himself.

Couldn't escape his thoughts.

It was madness to have trusted her. Madness to have cared.

They hadn't signed the prenup and they had had sex. But she was cheating on him, still seeing Alejandro. It was within his rights to send her away. But ending it with Emmeline wouldn't be a small thing. It would be a huge crisis, personally and politically. But once she was gone, and once the shock of the news had worn off, people would move on. He'd move on.

But when Zale imagined her leaving, when he imagined her gone, he didn't feel relief.

He felt…pain.

Loss.

Her fault, he thought. The hollow emptiness within him, this sense of loss, was her fault. She was a witch, not a princess, and she'd cast a spell on him.

But it was a spell he had to break. Sooner than later.

And so he ran harder, ran faster, leaving the track to do tortuous wind sprints down the center of the field, again and again, pushing himself for an hour, running until his legs shook, and his heart pounded and he couldn't catch his breath.

Finally, finally his mind was calm. His thoughts were quiet. Yes, his chest still ached, but now it was due to exhaustion not emotion. And he could handle that.

In the Queen's Chambers, Hannah paced the sitting room for a half hour after he left her, in case he should change his mind and return. He didn't.

After thirty minutes she went to his rooms but he wasn't there, either. She returned to her room, sank onto the small pink silk couch and picked up one of the French fashion magazines Lady Andrea had bought but she couldn't read, or even look at the pictures.

She wanted to fix things with Zale, make amends

somehow, but he didn't return to their rooms or summon her, and the afternoon slipped away and then evening came and the maids and footmen slipped in and out of rooms turning on lamps and building fires.

Numb, Hannah watched Celine build the fire in her sitting room's hearth with the pink marble surround. She listened to the pop and crackle as the dry kindling caught, and fed the bigger logs until flames danced and licked making the fire bright. But even with the fire's warmth next to her, Hannah remained chilled.

What if this was her last day here?

What if Zale sent her away?

What if he was making plans this very moment to put her on a plane?

Her stomach heaved and acid rose up in her throat. She couldn't leave, not like this. She had to see him. Had to make him understand. Hannah left the sofa even as the thought hit her—

What was she to do to make him understand?

That she'd tricked him, yes, but she'd had good intentions…?

Or that she'd deliberately deceived him because she'd fallen in love with him at first sight?

Hannah sank back down on the sofa cushion knowing she could never confess any of that.

Knowing she could never make any of this okay. Some things were too bad, too horrible to forgive.

When seven o'clock rolled around and Zale still hadn't put in an appearance or sent word about dinner, Hannah ate the meal Celine brought for her on one of the silver trolley tables they sent up from the kitchen.

At nine o'clock Celine asked Hannah if she'd like help changing into her gown and robe for bed.

Hannah shook her head. "Not yet," she answered huskily. "But there's no need for you to stay. I can change later when I'm ready. I know where everything is."

"You're certain, Your Highness?"

Hannah winced at the Highness part, feeling anything but royal. "Very certain. Good night, Celine. Sleep well."

At ten Hannah had had enough of sitting, waiting, worrying. She had to do something. Take action of some sort. Move. Walk. Find Zale.

Find Zale. Yes, that's what she needed to do. Immediately.

Ignoring the uniformed guards posted outside her room and throughout the palace, she went downstairs to the wing that contained his suite of offices—his library and office space, as well as adjoining rooms for secretaries and various assistants. But he wasn't there. The rooms were dark, the doors locked.

Where else would Zale be at ten o'clock at night? With his brother maybe?

Hannah returned to the family wing but on reaching Tinny's suite, she discovered it dark and Mrs. Daum in her nightgown and robe as it was Mrs. Sivka's night off.

Hannah stood on the grand staircase, confused. A footman approached her. "Is there something you're looking for, Your Highness?" he asked.

She struggled to hold her smile. "Yes, His Majesty. I seem to have misplaced him."

The footman appeared truly apologetic. "I'm sorry, Your Highness. I have not seen him, but I can certainly ask and see if someone knows His Majesty's whereabouts."

"That would be wonderful. Thank you."

"And will you be in your rooms, Your Highness?"

"Yes."

Fifteen minutes later Krek knocked on her door, arriving with the message that His Majesty hadn't gone out, nor was he with his brother, or in his private gym, but most definitely somewhere in the palace. Just where, no one knew.

It wasn't until Krek left that Hannah thought she

knew where Zale would be. The parapet. Where they'd had lunch today. Hadn't he said he liked to walk there when he had things on his mind or wanted to be alone?

Hannah took a soft velvet blue cloak from the dressing room and left her room to head downstairs, walking quickly through the now deserted grand rooms and corridors of the palace for the old castle keep.

The lights were dim in this part of the palace and her footsteps echoed eerily loud in the medieval hall as she searched for the right hallway that would lead to the tower stairs. But finally she found the stone arch and the circular staircase that wound to the top of the tower.

A guard was at the top of the stairs in front of the door, but he bowed and immediately opened it for her.

Hannah sucked in a quick breath at the chill in the air as she stepped into the night. It was a clear night and the lights of the city below played off the bright stars overhead.

She drew her dark blue velvet cloak closer and set off, walking along the high thick wall in search of Zale, imagining all the people who must have walked the same path in the eight hundred years since the castle was built.

She imagined the worries people must have had, the hopes and dreams, as well as the pain. In eight hundred years, politics, fashion and technology had changed, but the human heart hadn't.

"What are you doing?"

It was Zale's voice, coming from the dark and she jumped and turned, peering uneasily into the night. "Where are you?"

He moved away from the shadowed wall and into the open. Moonlight silhouetted his tall frame and lit his profile. "Here."

She couldn't read his expression but his voice was hard, his tone impatient. For a moment her courage wavered and then she gathered her strength and pushed on. "I am so sorry you had to hear any of that earlier, but it isn't what you think. It wasn't Alejandro. I haven't spoken to him since Palm Beach and even then, there was nothing." The words tumbled from her, one after the other, hoping somehow to get through to him.

He wasn't listening, though. "I don't care," he said brusquely.

"But I do, which is why I had to find you." She took a deep breath, nervously crushing the soft velvet fabric between her fingers. "I know I haven't been easy. I know I'm not the woman you wanted. And I wish I had been. I wish I could be the right woman, the one that could make everything perfect for you—"

"I don't need perfect," he interrupted roughly. "But I also won't tolerate dishonesty or deceit."

"I'm sorry. I am. But you must know that since I arrived I've only wanted one thing, and that is you."

He made a sound of disgust.

She moved toward him. "I mean it, Zale. There is no one else for me. I need you to believe me."

"Emmeline," he said warningly.

She ignored the threat in his voice. "I hate it that you're angry. Please forgive me—"

"Em—"

She cut off his protest by rising on tiptoe to kiss him. His lips were cold, rigid beneath hers but she couldn't give up, couldn't not try. And so she kissed him slowly, sweetly, reaching up to clasp his face between her hands. She could feel the rasp of his beard against her palms and the gradual warming of his mouth beneath hers.

And then he was kissing her back, hard, almost aggressively. She welcomed the punishing pressure of his mouth on hers, and in an instant the kiss exploded into something hot and hungry and fierce. Zale dragged a hand into her hair and knotted the silken strands around his fingers, drawing her head back to give him better access to her mouth. He parted her lips, his tongue plundering the soft recesses of her mouth.

He kissed her until her head spun and little stars danced before her eyes, kissing her senseless, kissing her until he was all and everything.

He pushed her back, pressing her against the cold stone wall, as his hands took hers, trapping them above her head, holding her immobile. "This isn't working," he said, leaning into her, his voice a rasp in her ear. "We don't work."

She could feel the warmth of his fingers wrapped around her slender wrists and the pressure of his hips grinding against hers. His hard, broad chest crushed her breasts and his knee pressed between her thighs, rubbing against her most sensitive place, and she felt absolutely no fear. Just pleasure. And desire.

She needed him. Wanted him. Wanted him even when he was savage and furious and intent on punishing her because he'd never hurt her. He'd always protect her. Even if it was from himself.

"But we do work," she answered. "At least this part does…when we're together like this."

"But sex, even great sex, doesn't make a marriage work. There has to be more. I want more." His voice was hard, sharp, and yet his head dipped and he kissed the corner of her mouth and then her soft lower lip.

"But we could have more," she protested, tipping her head back, eyes closing, as his lips traveled down the side of her neck setting her skin and body on fire.

"Yes, more drama," he answered, lips at the base of her throat, breath warm on the small hollow there. "More lies. But I can't do it. I won't."

"You promised me four days, Zale. We still have two days. Give me those days—"

"No."

"Please."

"Absolutely not."

"But isn't the Amethyst & Ice Ball tomorrow night? I know it's a huge fundraiser of the year for your personal charity. Won't it seem strange to not have me there?"

"It'd be worse trying to get through the evening acting like I like you."

Hannah flinched.

He released her and moved back a step, setting her free. "That was harsh, and I hate being cruel, but, Emmeline, we both know that you are not right for me, or good for me."

She realized then she was fighting a losing battle. Zale was finished with her. He did intend to send her away. And maybe this was the right thing to happen. Maybe this was the way it was to end.

She could leave in the morning and Zale would never know the truth…he'd never know that it wasn't Emmeline who was here, but Hannah. He'd never have to know he'd been deceived.

He turned his back on her, moving to the stone balustrade to look out over the city that glimmered with light. "I'm tired," he said after a moment. "Tired of talking. Tired of arguing. Tired of trying to make this work."

She could feel his exhaustion, too. It was in his voice, the slump of his shoulders, the bite of his words. "I understand."

"I will phone your father in the morning and tell him we've realized it won't work. I'll tell him it was a mutual decision and that our differences were just too great to overcome."

"Okay."

He looked at her from over his shoulder. "It's better this way, doing it now, instead of waiting until the last minute to cancel the wedding."

"I agree."

He dropped his head, closed his eyes, fingers digging into the stone wall. "So why does it feel like hell?"

A lump filled her throat and her eyes burned.

"Because despite our differences, we did have feelings for each other."

He drew a slow, heavy breath. "I'm sorry."

She went to him, and wrapped her arms around his waist, pressing her cheek to his back. "It's my fault. It's you that needs to forgive me."

He covered her hands with one of his. "It's late," he said roughly. "We should go to bed. The morning will be here soon enough."

"Can I sleep with you tonight?"

"That's just asking for trouble."

She kissed his back. Zale was warm and felt so good. But then everything about him was strong. Solid. Like the tough Texas men she'd known growing up, men with integrity, men who understood honor. "I won't cause trouble," she whispered. "I just want to be near you. Just want to sleep with you one last time."

"I won't change my mind, Emmeline. You'll still leave in the morning."

"I will."

He was silent so long she was sure he was going to refuse her, but then he lifted her hand to his mouth, pressed a kiss to her palm. "Then we'll spend our last night together and say our goodbyes in the morning."

They made love in his big bed with the brocade fabric panels down creating a cocoon for just the two of them. It was as if the rest of the world had fallen away and they were the only two who existed.

In the darkness Zale loved her slowly, holding back his own orgasm until he'd brought her to a climax, once and then again. Tonight there was a sweetness in their lovemaking, a poignancy in every kiss and caress. Closing her eyes, Hannah savored his hard body stretched over hers, his skin so warm and delicious to touch.

When she came a second time, her heart seemed to shatter along with her body and it was all she could do to hold back the tears, and keep him from feeling her pain. The pain was considerable.

She loved him, loved him, loved him and he'd never know it.

Tears burned beneath her lids and she shuddered in his arms, her body rippling with aftershocks even as her heart exploded with fresh pain.

Forgive me, Zale, she whispered silently, kissing his chest, just above where his heart would be.

Forgive me for not being who you needed me to be.

* * *

Zale couldn't sleep even though his body was spent. His mind wouldn't turn off. His thoughts raced. His chest ached.

Zale had always needed order. He did not do well with uncertainty. For him, ambivalence was akin to chaos. And chaos was a synonym for loss.

Loss of peace.

Loss of focus.

Loss of control.

And Zale needed control. He needed to be in control. Always. And the few times he wasn't in control terrible things happened, things with a tragic outcome.

Stephen's leukemia.

His parents' crash.

Tinny's seizures.

No, control was everything. Which is why he'd trained so hard in his sport. He knew that if he worked hard, relentlessly hard, he would be successful. He knew he had talent, but it was his commitment that drove him to the top. And it hadn't been by chance. His success was the direct result of drive, discipline and sacrifice.

He had put in the work and was rewarded.

He'd made the necessary sacrifices and earned peace of mind.

It was basic. Straightforward. Black and white.

But with Emmeline it was different. With Emmeline his emotions were chaotic. Primitive.

He felt wild around her. Fierce. As if he was barely clinging to control. Lately he wanted to grab her by the hair and haul her caveman-style to his lair and keep her there just for him. Even now he longed to lock her up, secure her, take away all the uncertainty.

Maybe then he'd be comfortable.

Maybe.

Hannah suddenly sighed, and murmuring something unintelligible in her sleep, pressed herself closer to his side, snuggling against the warmth of his chest as if that was the only place to be.

And just like that, he felt a hot, wrenching pain.

How could he love her? How could he—even now—want to hold her?

CHAPTER THIRTEEN

I T TOOK Hannah just a moment after waking to realize she was alone. Stretching out a hand to the space near her the sheets were cool.

Zale had been gone for a while.

The realization sent her heart tumbling and she rolled onto her stomach and buried her face in her pillow. It was morning. Zale was gone. And she'd be leaving here now.

Sometime in the next half hour or hour, she'd pack her things and say her goodbyes.

The idea of saying goodbye to Zale, though, made her heartsick.

She loved him but would leave him.

How was this right? How was it fair?

And how would Zale say goodbye to her? Would he come to her room and say goodbye there? Or would he meet her at the door? Or would he refuse to see her, and say nothing at all?

Hannah's heart contracted, her chest aching with the pressure and pain. *But you can't cry,* she told herself. *You must keep it together for Zale's sake. You must stay calm until you're gone.*

And she would stay calm. She'd focus on the future, on returning to her life, her own life, the life of an ordinary twenty-five-year-old woman working to pay her bills, make her car payment and cover her rent.

She once liked being ordinary, and she'd always loved her independence and autonomy. She'd enjoyed working and then coming home at night to her apartment, and curling up on the sofa and watching her favorite shows and reading her favorite books.

She could do this, she repeated, throwing back the covers to face her day.

Hannah had barely finished her shower in her bathroom in the Queen's Chambers when Lady Andrea came knocking on the door to discuss Hannah's day with her.

"It's going to be a busy day with the ball tonight," Lady Andrea said, consulting her calendar with the scrawl of events and notes. "You'll join His Majesty for morning coffee in his office, and then directly after you'll have a fitting with Monsieur Pierre who has flown in this morning with your gown for tonight's Amethyst & Ice Ball."

So that's how this would play out, Hannah

thought, unable to speak. He was summoning her to his office where he'd say a few brief words and then have her shown to the door. How perfectly professional. How wonderfully regal. "Thank you," she said. "I'll dress quickly."

"I'm not supposed to say anything," Lady Andrea said, dropping her voice, "but I've seen the ball-room. The decorations are breathtaking. The entire room has been transformed into a winter wonder-land with floor-to-ceiling ice sculptures."

Hannah didn't care about the ball. She wouldn't be there. But she did care about Zale. She cared very much about saying goodbye, and handling herself right. She had to keep it together. Had to be as calm and controlled in Zale's study as possible.

Twenty minutes later, Hannah found herself seated in Zale's personal study, a room lined with floor-to-ceiling books that made her think of a library, sipping a cup of coffee in a chair across from Zale's desk, wishing he'd speak.

He'd barely looked at her since she arrived a few minutes ago. Nor had he touched his coffee. Instead he stared at a spot on his desk, fingers drumming on the rich polished wood.

"Did you sleep well?" he finally spoke, breaking the unbearable silence.

She nodded. "Yes, thank you."

"Yesterday I was very upset. I overheard you on the phone and felt betrayed—"

"It's okay, Zale. I understand. I'm not going to make a scene—"

"I owe you an apology," he interrupted tersely. "I had it all wrong. You were telling me the truth. You weren't speaking to Alejandro."

She felt a shiver of alarm. "How do you know?"

"He was badly injured in a polo accident yesterday in Buenos Aires. He was in surgery for hours, and he remains unconscious in intensive care." He finally looked at her, his expression blank, his jaw hard. "I imagine you already knew that—"

"I didn't."

He looked away, swallowed hard. "I'm sorry, Emmeline. I know you have…strong…feelings for him."

She stared at her hands, fingers interlocked. "I'm sorry he was hurt, but I'm not in love with him."

"No?"

She shook her head and lifted it to meet his gaze. "How could I, when I care so much about you?"

For a long moment he searched her eyes before taking a deep breath. "You still do? Even though last night I was determined to throw you out?"

Her lips curved into a tremulous smile. "Yes."

He looked pale and tense and unhappy. "I'm sorry. I should have trusted you."

Guilt clawed at her. She struggled to hang on to her smile. "Mistakes happen."

"Can you forgive me?"

"Yes."

"And will you please stay? I don't want to host the ball tonight without you at my side."

"Yes. Absolutely. I'd love to be there with you."

"Thank you." He sounded relieved but his expression remained grim. "And in that case, I'm to send you straight back to your room for a final fitting for tonight's ball gown."

She nodded, forced another smile and quietly slipped away.

He watched her leave, listened as the door closed soundlessly behind her.

For a moment he felt strangely bereft. Hollow and empty and alone. He didn't like it.

He'd liked having her in his study. He enjoyed her company. Loved having her around.

She'd said last night that she knew she wasn't the woman he'd wanted, but she was wrong. She was exactly what he wanted. Now he just needed to prove it to her.

It was time he stopped trying to control everything so much. Time to stop defining everything as black or white. Could he open a little? Grow a little? Change for her?

Yes.

He pictured her sleeping so trustfully in his arms last night and he wanted that every night. He wanted a life with her, a future together. Marriage and babies and everything that went with it.

Across the palace in the Queen's Chambers, Hannah stood in her dressing room on the small, low stool in a thin white Grecian gown that wouldn't zip closed, her image caught reflected in the numerous mirrors.

And no one said anything.

Not Lady Andrea who sat in the corner with her notebook. Or Camille and Teresa who stood against the far wall. Or Celine, who hovered behind Anton Pierre, the designer from Paris who'd just flown in that morning hand carrying the two commissioned gowns—the ball gown for tonight's gala and the wedding dress for Saturday's ceremony.

No one spoke because what could anyone say?

The thin, slim chiffon gown should have cascaded effortlessly in an elegant column of white. Instead the fabric rode up in Hannah's armpits and the back wouldn't zip. Turning her head, Hannah could see her thin bra strap across her back and even that looked tight.

"Suck in your stomach," Anton Pierre said, tugging hard on the zipper of the gown, lips pursed, expression critical.

"I am," Hannah answered, wincing a little as the zipper pinched her back, catching at her skin.

"More," he insisted.

She yelped as he zipped another bit of skin. "Ouch, stop! Stop. That hurts."

Anton threw his hands up in displeasure. "If this gown is too tight, your wedding gown isn't going to fit, either. Your breasts and hips are huge, Your Highness. What have you been eating?"

"Not a lot," Hannah answered, knowing she'd actually lost weight in the past week, at least five pounds.

"Nonsense. I think you're bingeing on butter and bon bons, Your Highness. I've dressed you for years and you've always asked me to tell you the truth. So I'm telling you the truth. You're fat. You have chub." He grabbed an inch on her back near her bra strap and pinched. "This is bad. You must lose ten pounds quickly—immediately—or you won't be wearing my wedding gown. It's made for a princess, not a midfielder."

"Get out!" Zale's voice thundered through the

dressing room, rattling a mirror on one wall. He looked huge and violently angry as he gestured toward the door. "Get out, Pierre, before I personally throw you out."

Then he turned on Lady Andrea. "How dare you allow a designer to speak to Her Highness that way? Where is your loyalty? Where is your allegiance? Perhaps you need to pack up your things, too, and join Monsieur Pierre on his plane home."

Lady Andrea covered her mouth, holding back a sob. "Your Majesty, forgive me. I was just about to intervene—"

"When?" He interrupted. "I stood outside the door listening. I heard it all. When were you going to intervene? How far did you intend to let it go?"

Lady Andrea shook her head and wiped away tears that were falling fast and furious.

"That's all the answer I need," Zale retorted. "Pack your things."

He turned to Celine, Camille and Teresa next. "And you three? What is your excuse? Why did none of you protect Her Highness?"

Celine's eyes were huge in her face. "I should have, Your Majesty. I wanted to. But I was scared."

"Why?"

Celine glanced at Hannah and then back to Zale. "I didn't think it was my place because Monsieur

Pierre is so famous and Princess Emmeline's favorite designer..." Her voice drifted off and she pressed her hands together. "Should I pack my things, too?"

Zale looked at Hannah who still stood on the stool with the gaping chiffon gown clutched to her chest. His jaw jutted, eyes blazed and for a moment he just looked at her, expression impossible to read, then turned back to Celine. "I will let Her Highness make that decision. But I want all of you to leave us now. I'd like to speak to Princess Emmeline alone."

The staff escaped from the dressing room and closed the outer door to the suite.

Zale crossed to the stool where Hannah was standing. "Give me your hand."

She did and he helped her step off the stool and onto the ground.

"Turn around," he instructed.

She did and he drew the zipper down so she could step from the dress.

"How could you let him speak to you that way?" He gritted, his features hard, his expression savage.

"I'm supposed to be thin," she whispered.

"Utter nonsense. You are perfect. I wouldn't change one thing about you."

Her eyes burned and she blinked. "Yes, but fashion designers prefer very slim models. Clothes look better that way."

"I couldn't care less about clothes. I care about you."

Her heart staggered a bit inside her chest. "You do?"

"Can't you tell? I haven't kept my hands off you since you arrived."

"I figured you had a healthy sex drive."

"I do, but I've had no problem managing it until I met you."

She smiled crookedly. "You still make that sound like a problem."

"It is. I pride myself on my self-control but you have challenged it, and challenged me, at every turn. But I'm glad. It's made me realize just how strong my feelings are for you." He drew a rough breath, his expression darkening all over again. "My God, how dare Pierre talk to you that way? I nearly thrashed him! I still want to go after him, teach him a thing or two."

He did sound angry, crazy angry, which was so not Zale Patek, King of Cool. "But what about tonight's ball? I need something to wear."

"We'll get that one altered," he said. "I know a Raguvian designer who puts Anton Pierre to shame."

"You think she can fix it?"

"Not just fix. Eva will improve the design." He looked at her, shook his head. "She'll take what I think is a rather boring dress and will make it extraordinary. You are an extraordinary woman and deserve no less."

Her heart skipped.

He'd just called her extraordinary. The words her father had used for her late mother. The words she'd always wanted to hear. "Thank you," she said, her voice breaking.

He reached for her, pulling her into his arms. His head dipped and his mouth covered hers, lips traveling slowly, leisurely over hers, drawing a hot, hungry response.

Hannah gloried in his warmth, and slipped her hands up his broad chest to wrap her arms around his neck.

His hands moved to her hips and he molded her against him. He was hard and hungry for her but after another long, melting kiss he pushed her gently away. "If I don't make some calls now, and track Eva down, you won't have a dress to wear tonight."

She gave him a naughty smile. "That's okay. I'll go naked."

"The hell you will," he said on a growl.

Hannah laughed as he swatted her backside and was still smiling after he left and she threw herself onto her bed.

She stretched happily, recalling how Zale had swept into the dressing room and ordered Pierre out. It was like a scene from a movie. Zale Patek, rushing in on his white stallion to save the lady in distress.

Hannah's smile faded as she thought of Lady Andrea. Poor Andrea. Hannah wasn't sure that Andrea deserved to be fired. Monsieur Pierre was intimidating. No one knew how to handle him… well, no one but Zale. Hannah decided she'd talk to Zale and ask him to hire Andrea back.

Hannah was still lounging on the bed when her phone in the nightstand drawer buzzed with an incoming message.

Hannah knew it was from Emmeline. She could feel it in her bones. And this time she didn't want to know what Emmeline had to say.

A minute passed. And then another. Finally, reluctantly, Hannah retrieved the phone and opened it.

It was from Emmeline. The text was brief.

I'm not coming to Raguva. The wedding is off. Once you leave I'll break the news to Zale. Text me when you're gone. Sorry.

Hannah blinked, read it again and when the words were the same, she felt everything tilt and slide, crashing into disaster.

It had all been for naught.

Emmeline wasn't going to marry Zale. Zale would be embarrassed and angry beyond measure.

She read the message again. And then again. But each time it was the same.

Emmeline wasn't coming. She wouldn't be marrying Zale after all. And Hannah had to go.

Little spots danced before Hannah's eyes. She had to go. Had to leave.

A knock sounded on the bedroom door. "Your Highness?" It was Celine. "Can I come in?"

Hannah couldn't speak. Breathe, breathe, she told herself, air bottled in her lungs.

"Your Highness?"

Tears filled Hannah's eyes. It had happened. She had to leave. But she couldn't go tonight, not hours before the ball. She couldn't humiliate Zale like that. No, she'd go in the morning, first thing tomorrow.

"Yes," she called out at last, her voice faint, strangled. "Please, come in, Celine."

Celine opened the door and saw Hannah sitting on the bed wiping away tears. "Is everything all right, Your Highness?"

"Everything's great."

CHAPTER FOURTEEN

THE ball was less than three hours away, and Hannah was getting a Swedish massage on a special table in her dressing room. The lights were dimmed, candles burned and soft instrumental music played. It was supposed to be a treat, something Zale had arranged for her, but Hannah was too keyed-up to enjoy it.

"Take a nice slow, deep breath," the masseuse said soothingly, rubbing fragrant lavender oil into Hannah's tense shoulders. "Now exhale. Slowly, slowly, Your Royal Highness. Good. Now again."

Hannah tried to do as she was told, she did, but it was hard to relax when everything inside her was tied up in knots.

She hated Emmeline right now. Hated Emmeline for what she'd done. Hannah should have never come here. She shouldn't have ever agreed to play acting for an afternoon much less a week.

If only she hadn't gotten on the plane. If only she'd refused to continue the charade at that point.

But she hadn't. She'd been too worried, afraid that the princess was facing a crisis all alone.

"Your Highness," the masseuse said gently, but firmly, kneading Hannah's shoulders. "Let go of everything. Just focus on your breathing. Focus on feeling good for the next half hour."

And somehow, beneath the magic hands of the masseuse, Hannah did relax, shutting everything from her mind for the next thirty minutes, but once she was in her bathroom, showering off the oil and shampooing her hair, the anxiety returned.

So how did she fix this with Zale? There had to be something she could do…some magical fix, but standing in the shower, hot water pounding down, Hannah could think of nothing.

Hannah had always prided herself on being able to handle whatever her difficult, demanding boss, Sheikh Koury, sent her way. The Sheikh had been through a dozen secretaries before he found Hannah who could speak four languages fluently and handle the endless and challenging work he tossed her way.

No matter what he dropped in her lap, she handled it with aplomb. Arrange an environmental awareness meeting with the world's leading oil executives? No problem.

Plan activities for the oil executives' wives, many

of whom had to be segregated from men? Hannah didn't even blink.

Organize an international polo tournament in Dubai? Then move it to Buenos Aires? And provide transportation for all players and horses? Consider it done.

Hannah loved puzzles and thrived on good challenges, but the one thing she couldn't do, and the one thing she was desperate to do, was protect Zale from what was to come.

The truth.

Eva, the Raguvian designer, had reworked the ball gown for Hannah, changing the design from a simple off-white column dress, to a shimmering chiffon gown with jeweled embroidered flowers unfurling across the bodice and to bloom down one hip in a profusion of purple and amethyst jewel petals that reached her feet.

She wore pale gold sling-back heels with more jewels at the toe, and her blond hair was piled high on her head and held in place with glittering citrine and amethyst hairpins. Rectangular rose-gold, diamond and amethyst earrings hung from her ears, a cuff circled her wrist, and on Zale's arm she felt like a princess.

"You're a goddess tonight," Zale said as they

paused inside the ballroom doors and took in the glittering winter wonderland anchored by a dozen massive ice columns. "More beautiful than any woman has a right to be."

She flushed with pleasure, heat radiating out from the tight coil of desire in her belly to the tingle in her fingers and toes. "I don't know what to say."

Zale was dressed in black coat and tails, white shirt, white vest and tie and looked devastatingly attractive, especially when he smiled, and he was smiling now. "Just say thank you."

And then they were being announced and swept into the immense white and gold palace ballroom that glittered with floor-to-ceiling ice sculptures and potted trees brought in just for the occasion. The trees' white, frosted limbs were covered by strands of miniature white lights and the only spot of color in the glittering white room was the ladies' elegant gowns in shades of purple, violet and lavender.

Zale and Hannah circled the room on their way to the head table, Zale's hand resting lightly on her back. She could feel the heat from Zale's hand and she shivered as exquisite sensation raced through her. There was something about his touch…something in the way her body responded to him that made her feel so alive.

"What do you think?" he asked as they took their places on the platform, several feet higher than the rest of the room.

"It's absolutely magical. I feel like a princess from a fairy tale."

He grinned. "Which one?"

"Cinderella." She reached down to lightly touch one of the jeweled blossoms on her waist. "Eva waved her magic wand and voilà! I'm a princess at your ball."

Uniformed footmen filled their tall, slender flutes with champagne. Zale lifted his flute. "To my princess," he said, a half smile playing at his lips.

"To my king," she replied, clinking the rim of her glass to his.

They drank and the champagne's tiny bubbles fizzed in her mouth and the cold liquid warmed as it went down.

"Have all Raguvian kings married royalty?" Hannah asked, setting her flute back on the table. "Has no one married a...commoner?"

"Only once in the past two hundred years and he gave up his throne to marry her."

"Why is a blue-blood bride essential?"

"Our monarchy grew out of a tribal kingship that

spanned nearly a thousand years, and the Raguvian people have fought hard to preserve the monarchy, although today we are—like Brabant—a constitutional monarchy."

Hannah knew the differences between monarchies from working for Sheikh Koury.

There were absolute monarchies like those in the Middle East—Brunei, Saudi Arabia, Qatar—and then there were constitutional monarchies like those in Belgium, Sweden, Monaco and the United Kingdom. A constitutional monarchy gave a king power as defined by each country's constitution.

Her brow furrowed. "Does it actually say in your constitution that you must marry a royal?"

"Yes."

"You couldn't marry a commoner?"

"Not without relinquishing the throne."

"And you wouldn't do that?"

"I could not."

She noticed his word choice. It wasn't that he wouldn't. He couldn't. "Why couldn't you?"

"I could never be selfish enough to put my needs before that of my country."

She ran a fingertip around the base of the flute stem, watching the tiny gold bubbles of champagne rise to the surface and pop.

Even if Zale wanted Hannah Smith, he wouldn't

choose her. Even if Zale should love her, he wouldn't keep her. "Have you ever dated a commoner?" she asked, voice breaking.

"All my girlfriends were commoners." His lips curled, slightly mocking. "You are my first princess."

And she wasn't even a real princess, either.

Her heart grew even heavier during dinner. It didn't help that when Zale looked at her, she lost track of time. In his eyes there was just now, only now, and right now she was happy. Lucky. Good.

Suddenly Zale was standing and extending his hand to her. "Your Highness," he said, his smile warming his eyes, warming her, making her feel so very alive. But then, he was so very alive. "May I have this dance?"

She looked up into his lean face with the strong brow, firm mouth and uncompromising chin and a frisson of feeling raced through her. "Yes."

She rose, putting her hand into his, inhaled as sensation exploded inside her, making her body go hot and cold. Again. He'd done it again. Made her want, made her feel, making her aware of just how much she loved him.

Zale led her toward the dance floor as the orchestra started playing the first notes of an achingly familiar love song she'd played endlessly on her guitar growing up.

"Your favorite song," Zale murmured as he pulled her into his arms and close to his tall lean frame.

Hot emotion rushed through her. How did he know?

And then as his hand settled low on her back, his warmth scorching her through her thin gown, she remembered he meant Emmeline.

Of course he meant Emmeline. But Emmeline wasn't coming. It all ended tonight.

For a moment she couldn't breathe, suffocated by crushing pain.

Early tomorrow morning she'd slip away, leaving him a note. He'd hate her when he found the note. She'd never forgive herself for deceiving him, either.

"You're a good dancer," she whispered.

"That's because you're my perfect partner."

Eyes burning, heart on fire, she tipped her head back and was immediately lost in Zale's eyes. She loved his face. Loved everything about him far too much. "You are full of compliments tonight, Your Majesty."

He smiled at her. "I'm happy."

He did look happy. His light brown eyes glowed. "I'm glad."

"Marry me, Emmeline."

"I thought we were?"

"I'm proposing again so we can start over. Start fresh. This isn't about our families or our countries. This is about us. Will you marry me?"

Her eyes filled with tears. She blinked to clear her vision. "You're sweeping me off my feet."

"It's what I should have done from the beginning."

"I had no idea you were such a romantic."

His steady gaze held hers. "So is that a yes, Your Highness? Or do you need time to think about it?"

Her chest ached. How could she say no? How could she ever refuse him anything? "Yes."

He smiled, a great boyish smile that lit his face and made him look utterly irresistible. "Thank God. For a moment I thought you intended to leave me standing at the altar."

He was teasing. Trying to be funny. But Hannah shivered, chilled by reality.

Zale felt the goose bumps on her arms and drew her closer. "Cold?"

"A little."

He held her even more snugly against him and she pressed her cheek closer to his jacket, her ear resting on his chest just above his heart. And remembered Cinderella.

In *Cinderella,* at the stroke of midnight the magic ended. The glass coach turned back into a pumpkin. Cinderella's gown became rags. And Cinderella became no one.

The song was ending and Zale lifted her hand to his mouth, kissing her fingers. "Thank you."

She looked up into his face, that handsome face, which owned every bit of her heart. "Have you ever been in love?"

"Yes."

"She was a commoner?"

He nodded.

"What happened?"

His jaw tightened. "My parents died and I became king."

She stared up at him. "You gave her up?"

He nodded again and she exhaled in a rush. Tenderly Zale brushed a wisp of hair from her flushed cheek. "It hurt," he admitted, "but it was meant to be. Because if I hadn't ended it with her, I wouldn't be here with you."

Zale saw her cheeks turn pink and her blue eyes deepen, a sheen of tears making the color look like sapphires, a perfect complement to the jewels in her hair and at her ears.

She'd never looked more beautiful, and yet she

hadn't been this emotional, or fragile, since their engagement party. But he understood her exhaustion. It had been a hard night without either of them getting a lot of sleep.

"I see some friends across the room," he said, taking her hand. "Let's go say hello."

All evening he'd introduced her to different people he thought she should know—members of his cabinet, members of parliament, influential men and women from all over the world. But now he was taking her to old friends, close friends, people Emmeline loved.

Crossing the ballroom they joined the Greek prince, Stavros Kallas, and his bride of one year, the stunning Greek-English heiress, Demi Nowles. Prince Stavros was a first cousin of Zale's, their mothers were half sisters and Stavros had been a friend of Emmeline's since childhood.

When Stavros had proposed to Demi Nowles after a whirlwind engagement, no one had been happier than Emmeline who'd socialized with Demi for years. One year they'd been the inseparable dancing duo, hitting every exclusive nightclub on the Continent.

"I do believe you know these two," Zale said. "Perhaps *you* should introduce *me,* Your Highness?"

Emmeline didn't reply and glancing down at her he saw panic in her eyes.

"Your Highness," he prompted, gently, teasingly. "If you'd do me the honor…?"

Emmeline smiled, but her features were tight, and her expression looked frozen.

She extended a hand to Prince Stavros. "It's a pleasure," she said politely. "Good to see you again."

Stavros looked at Emmeline's hand, glanced at Zale and then back at Emmeline before slowly taking her hand. "Yes," he agreed uncomfortably. "You look well, Emmeline."

Zale frowned, and Demi watched the exchange, equally baffled.

For a moment Demi didn't seem to know what to do and then her expression suddenly cleared. "Oh, Emi, I get it now! You're making fun of those Americans and their strange manners. You were just there in Palm Beach for that polo tournament. Heard it was quite the crush."

"Yes, it was," Emmeline agreed pleasantly. "How long are you here for?"

Silence followed Emmeline's question, a most awkward silence, and even Demi's smooth brow furrowed. "Until the wedding, of course," Demi answered, perplexed. "Unless you've decided to replace me as one of your bridesmaids."

Again there was silence and Zale caught Stavros and Demi exchanging puzzled glances.

Zale reached for Emmeline's hand. She was trembling. He didn't understand what was happening.

"No," Emmeline answered, breaking the excruciating silence. She smiled but she looked alarmingly brittle. "Don't be ridiculous. How could I get married without you at my side?"

Stavros smiled. Demi hugged Emmeline. But Zale wasn't fooled. Something was wrong with Emmeline.

They moved on, just a short distance from Prince and Princess Kallas. "Are you all right?" Zale asked, his head bent to hers, his voice pitched low.

She swayed on her feet. "I don't feel well."

He slipped an arm around her waist to support her weight. "I can see that," he said, leading her through a narrow door hidden in the ballroom's ornate white and gold paneling, exiting the ballroom for a small cream room where he swept her into his arms and carried her to a chaise in the corner.

He settled her on the chaise and she lay still with her eyes closed, her lashes black crescents against her pallor. "Do you feel faint?" he asked.

She nodded.

"A little."

"What can I get for you?"

Tears seeped from beneath her lashes. "Nothing."

Zale summoned a footman. "Brandy and water," he said crisply.

The footman returned quickly and Zale carried the snifter of brandy to Emmeline. "Drink. It'll help."

She sat up, brushing away tears and took a sip, gasping a bit as the alcohol burned her throat.

He waited for her to take another sip before standing up. "How do you feel now?" he asked.

"Better."

But her teeth were chattering and she was still too pale.

Zale slipped his coat off and draped it around her shoulders before moving to stand in front of the fireplace. He stared into the cold hearth. "You didn't recognize them," he said bluntly. "You still don't know who they are."

She lifted her head, looked at him then, her blue eyes shadowed. "No. I don't."

"And you shook Stavros's hand. He's a childhood friend."

"I…embarrassed you."

"No. That's not the issue. I just don't understand. How can you not know them?"

She didn't answer, her head hung in shame.

But he didn't want shame. Nor did he want an apology. He wanted answers. "Are you on something? Taking something? Pills…uppers, downers, pain medicine?"

"No."

"Diet pills, or an appetite suppressant?"

"No."

"Snorting anything? Smoking anything?"

Her head jerked up and she gave him a horrified look. "No!"

"Then what?" His voice throbbed with emotion. "What the hell happened in there?"

"I'm tired, Zale. Confused. I haven't been sleeping much lately—"

"That doesn't hold up. You always travel. You are a globe-trotting royal, never long in the same place."

"But there's been so much stress. We've had problems and the wedding is just days from now—"

"I don't buy it. Not from you. You are Emmeline d'Arcy. You thrive on stress. So tell me what happened in there. Tell me why you're acting like this."

"I'm telling you but you're not listening."

"No. What you're telling me are lies. I can see

it in your face. You haven't told me the truth yet. And I want the truth."

Hand trembling, she reached for the brandy, took another sip and then set the glass back down. "Maybe you should sit."

His temper flared. "I prefer standing."

She nodded once, a small nod that said nothing and yet everything. "This isn't going to be easy."

"Please," he groaned impatiently. "Spare me the theatrics."

Her chin lifted and she looked up at him, expression blank. For a long moment she said nothing and then she shrugged. "I'm not Emmeline."

CHAPTER FIFTEEN

ZALE gritted his teeth. Not Emmeline? It was ridiculous. She was being ridiculous.

"This isn't a good time for drama," he said, striving to stay pleasant, and trying not to think of the three hundred and fifty guests in the ballroom awaiting their return. "We're throwing a party. A huge fundraiser. Until now it's been quite a success. Let's sort this out so we can return—"

"I'm not Emmeline," she repeated flatly, no emotion anywhere in her voice, her expression equally vacant. "I'm Hannah. Hannah Smith."

Again he felt that need to laugh but then he saw her face and finally understood she wasn't joking. She was serious.

Zale abruptly sat down. "What do you mean you're not Emmeline?"

"I've just been pretending," she whispered, hands clenched into a fist in her lap. "I was doing Emmeline a favor. I was only supposed to be her for a few hours while she went to see friends, but she never came back, and I got onto the plane and then I was here."

He stared at her in shock.

She'd lost her mind. She needed help. "I'll get you a doctor," he said gently. "We'll get you care—"

"I'm not sick," she interrupted, her voice low but steady. "Just very foolish. Inexcusably foolish. And I don't expect you to forgive me, but it's time you knew the truth."

She looked up at him, eyes bright, cheeks finally taking on some color. "I'm an American. I work in Dallas as a secretary for an Arab sheikh named Makin Al-Koury—"

"I know Sheikh Al-Koury. He just hosted the Palm Beach Polo Tournament."

"I organized the event." She drew a quick breath. "And that's where I met Her Highness, Princess Emmeline d'Arcy. We were mistaken for each other so often that she requested a meeting with me. The princess needed to take care of something and asked for my help—"

"To impersonate her?"

She nodded. "Her Highness said she would never be able to leave without a disguise, and so she left the hotel as me."

"Where was she going?"

"I don't know. She never told me. She just said

she needed to take care of something and she'd be back in a few hours." Hannah laced and unlaced her fingers. "But she never returned that day. Or the next. So here I am."

They never returned to the ballroom. The Amethyst & Ice Ball finished without them.

Instead Zale had Emmeline escorted back to the Queen's Chambers, his tuxedo jacket still draped across her shoulders. He headed to the parapet where he walked the tower for half an hour.

He didn't believe her. Couldn't.

Emmeline wasn't Emmeline but an American secretary named Hannah Smith?

Impossible.

There weren't two Emmelines in the world, and Emmeline d'Arcy was such a rare beauty, so distinctive that there couldn't be another woman who looked like her.

Or moved like her.

Or smiled like her.

Which meant that Emmeline wasn't well, and he needed to get her away from Raguva, away from the pressures of the palace, far from the wedding preparations and all the attention that came with both.

She needed rest and medical care and he'd make sure she got the help she needed.

Back downstairs he gave instructions for his jet to be prepared for an early morning departure. He sent for Krek and told his butler that he needed a suitcase packed. "I'm not sure how long I'll be gone…one week, two. See to it that Her Highness's maid packs for her, too."

Krek stood there a moment looking confused. "Pack another suitcase, Your Majesty?"

"No, Krek. She just needs one."

"But Her Highness went downstairs with a small suitcase a little while ago. Her maid found this on the floor in the living room. She must have dropped it on the way out." The butler reached into the pocket of his black pin-striped trousers and withdrew Emmeline's phone. "Perhaps you could give it to her when you see her?"

Zale took the phone, turning it over in his hand. The infamous phone. The source of so much tension.

Silent, gut hard, chest tight, Zale flipped the phone open to scroll through her in-box. Text from Emmeline.

Text from Emmeline.

Text from Emmeline.

His chest squeezed tighter. He drew a rough, unsteady breath as Krek quietly left. For a moment Zale wanted to hurl the phone across the room but instead he sat down in the nearest chair to read the messages. He went back to the very beginning and read them all, incoming as well as outgoing since he had time, because Emmeline, or Hannah, or whoever she said she was, wouldn't be going anywhere. The palace gates were always locked, and no one came or went without Zale's knowledge and permission.

Just as Krek said, Hannah had packed a suitcase, and changed into traveling clothes, but she couldn't get out of the palace. The gates were locked. The palace guard stood at attention. They refused to even make eye contact with her. She tried to persuade one guard and then another to open the gates but each one stared straight ahead as if she wasn't even there.

Hannah gave up pleading and sat down on the palace's front steps. It was a clear night, a cool night, and she was growing cold but she'd rather freeze to death on the steps than go back inside.

She was beginning to think she'd freeze to death, too, when Zale's very deep voice spoke on the top step behind her. "Hannah Smith, you have some explaining to do."

Her stomach plummeted. Goose bumps covered

her arms. Slowly she rose knowing that this next conversation with Zale would be horrendous.

She was right. He grilled her for hours, repeating the same questions over and over. It was three-thirty in the morning now and Zale was growing angrier by the minute.

"It's illegal what you've done," he said harshly after she finally fell silent, worn-out from talking, exhausted from trying to make him understand. "You've broken too many laws to count. You didn't just impersonate Princess Emmeline, you committed fraud as we well as perjury."

She stared at him dry-eyed, her body trembling from fatigue. "I *am* sorry."

"Not good enough."

"How can I make amends? I want to make amends."

"You can't," he answered brusquely. "And the more I think about it, the more certain I am that I should have you arrested. Locked up. Let you sit in jail for a couple of years—"

"*Zale.*"

But he couldn't be placated. "What sort of person are you? Who does what you did?"

"I was never supposed to come here. I'd never agreed to come—"

"But you did."

Hannah's shoulders twisted helplessly. "I kept thinking that any moment Emmeline would show up. Any moment she'd return and we'd switch places again and that would be that."

"What you did was a crime! It's a serious offense to enter the country under false pretenses, use a fake identity, interfere with state business. Any one of those would earn you a stiff prison sentence, but all three together?" He shook his head. "How could you do it?"

"I don't know." Hannah felt horrible, beyond horrible. "And there isn't a good excuse. I was stupid. Beyond stupid. And I knew I was in trouble once I got here but I didn't know how to put a stop to it. I liked you immediately. Fell for you hard—"

"Please don't go there."

"It's true. I fell for you at first sight. And I knew you weren't mine. I knew you belonged to Emmeline but she wouldn't come, and yet she wouldn't let me leave."

"So you decided to just stay and play princess, thinking no one would ever find out the truth?"

She bit her lip, unable to defend herself. Because yes, that's what she'd naively hoped.

Stupid, stupid, Hannah.

The silence hung between them, tense, agonizing, and then Zale turned away, making a rough sound in his throat. "To think I nearly fell in love with you. A fake. An impostor! My God, I even took you to my bed—"

"You can't blame me for that. You wanted to sleep with me, too!"

"Yes, because I thought you were mine. I thought you were to be my wife. I had no idea you were an American girl getting her thrills pretending to be my fiancée."

"It wasn't like that. I didn't want to betray you or Emmeline—"

"But you did, and you did come to my bed, and you enjoyed it." He went to her, tangled his hand in her hair and forced her face up to his. "Didn't you?"

Her jaw tightened and she stared up at him in mute fury. Zale saw the blaze of anger in her eyes and he welcomed it. Good, let her be angry. Let her hurt. Let her feel a tenth of his pain and shame.

To be tricked like that…

Played for a fool…

He'd never forgive her. Never.

Zale released her, disgusted with her, him, all of it. "So where is Emmeline now?" he demanded, taking a step away. "Why isn't she here?"

Hannah shook her head. "I don't know. She never said."

He turned his back on her, walked across the room toward the windows. The drapes had not been drawn against the night and the lights of the walled city twinkled below. "I have to call her father. Tell him what's happened. We'll need to let our guests know the wedding is off."

She knotted and unknotted her hands. "Can I do something?"

"Yes. You can go." He spoke without turning around, keeping his back to her. "I want you gone first thing in the morning, and I never want to see you again."

Hannah left before daybreak. This time the palace guard allowed her to leave and she walked through the palace gates and out onto the cobbled streets, her footsteps unsteady.

The worst had finally happened. Zale had found out the truth. He knew who she was now, knew Emmeline wasn't coming, and now she was free to return to her own life, resume her work, see her friends.

This is what she'd wanted. This is what her goal had been. And yes, she was sad now—shattered, actually—but eventually she'd be okay. Hannah knew she was tough. Resilient. And maybe one day if she was lucky, she'd fall in love again.

Reaching the old city center, Hannah went to the train station to purchase a ticket and discovered she didn't have enough money to get across Raguva much less out of the country as she'd left her credit cards in her hotel room in Palm Beach. She'd need her father to wire her money and get one of the secretaries at the office in Dallas to overnight her passport to her.

Hannah reached into her coat pocket to call her dad but her phone was missing. She searched the rest of her pockets before opening her small suitcase to check there. But no, nothing, which meant she must have left the phone at the palace or dropped it while walking into the city center.

Her heart fell as she imagined returning to the palace, only to be confronted by Zale.

She couldn't handle seeing him again. Couldn't handle his disappointment and anger.

Last night she'd felt like Cinderella at the ball—a beautiful princess dancing with the handsome king—and just like the fairy tale, today she was no one. She'd been tossed into the streets.

Exhausted, Hannah closed her suitcase and got to her feet and stood in the middle of the train station, wishing she had a fairy godmother who could come wave a magic wand and make everything good again.

But fairy godmothers didn't exist, and real life women like Hannah Smith had to sort out their problems and mistakes on their own.

Only her plight hadn't gone unnoticed. An old gentleman working at the station ticket counter left his booth and approached her, speaking a mixture of broken English and Raguvian. "Do you need help?"

She nodded, hating the lump in her throat. "I need to find a hotel, something cheap, for a night or two until my father can send money."

He pointed to a building across the street. "Nice and clean," he said, with a sympathetic smile. "And not too much money. Tell them Alfred sent you."

She shot him a grateful smile. "I will, thank you."

He nodded and watched her hurry across the plaza to the small hotel tucked into the stone building on the other side of the cobbled street.

The woman at the front desk seemed to be waiting for Hannah at the front door. She ushered her in and got her registered at the small reception desk in minutes before personally showing Hannah to her room, explaining through gestures and smiles how the small ancient television and room thermostat worked.

When Hannah told her she needed a phone to

make a collect call to the United States, the woman handed Hannah her own from her dress pocket.

But the phone operator couldn't reach Hannah's father for him to accept the collect call. They tried twice before Hannah gave up.

"You can try again later, as many times as you need," the front desk clerk assured her. "I will be here all day."

Hannah did try three more times, but each time she had the operator try to place the collect call, her father's answering machine picked up.

By the end of the day, Hannah had resigned herself to the fact that she'd be stuck in Raguva at least another day. If not longer.

For the first twenty-four hours after Hannah left, Zale wanted revenge. He fantasized about hunting Hannah down and making her suffer as he was suffering.

He was still angry the second day after she'd left, and plotted her downfall, but now when he imagined doing something to her, he was doing something to her body. Something...pleasurable.

He hated himself for even thinking of her, much less desiring her.

The fact that he could imagine taking pleasure

in her body baffled him after everything that had happened.

Why was he even thinking about her? How could he want her? She'd manipulated him and played him and he should hate her.

He didn't. He couldn't. Not when he loved her.

Zale ran a hand through his short hair, knowing he'd only been in love once before. It'd been six years ago when he'd lived in Madrid. She had been young, brilliant and vivacious, a breathtaking Spanish beauty, but when his parents had died he'd retired from football and ended their love affair, moved back to Raguva and never once looked back.

Zale knew how to move on without looking back. He knew how to be ruthless, relentless, hard.

And he'd force himself to be ruthless and hard now.

She was gone. And there would be no forgiveness. No second chances.

But when he pictured Hannah, he didn't want to be ruthless and hard.

On the third day Zale woke, even more angry and frustrated than when he went to bed.

He would find her. He would. He'd take her in his hands and make her pay.

But first he had to find her.

Zale spent the morning making inquiries before

turning to Krek at noon. Turns out he should have started with Krek as his butler already knew where Hannah could be found. "The Divok Hotel, Your Majesty, under the name of Hannah Smith."

Zale tried to hide his irritation. "How did you know where she was?"

"Her Highness is distinctive. Word quickly spread."

"No one told me."

"Everyone knew you were unhappy with her—"

"Does *everyone* know why?"

Krek shrugged vaguely. "Lovers' quarrel, something of that nature."

"They are aware the wedding has been called off?"

"Yes, Your Majesty, but they're all hoping that you'll come to your senses and forgive her so the wedding can be on again."

"It's not going to happen."

"Whatever you think is best, sir."

"Krek, I know you heard us fighting. I know you and half the palace must know the truth. She isn't Emmeline d'Arcy. She's an American impostor."

"Yes, Your Majesty."

"Krek."

The butler bowed. "Will you be going out, sir?"

Zale glowered at him. *"Yes."*

"Very good, sir."

Zale was annoyed that he'd be showing up at the unassuming Divok Hotel with full escort, but he couldn't very well go alone. He was a king. There was protocol. And safety was always an issue, even in his own country.

Zale waited in his armored car as his security guard checked out the hotel, securing the front and back entrances before allowing him inside.

The front desk clerk's welcome was effusive. Beaming and bowing, she showed him and four of his bodyguards up to the top floor, which was where she'd given Hannah Smith a room. "It's one of our best rooms," she said, "and every day I make sure she has fresh flowers."

Zale thanked the clerk for the kindness she'd shown Hannah Smith, and knocked on Hannah's door.

He waited a moment, gut tensing, and then knocked again. Finally she opened the door a crack and peered out, her long hair messy, her face pale with deep shadows beneath her eyes. The interior of her room was dark with the blinds still drawn although it was almost noon.

She blinked at him, obviously stunned but sleepy. "What are you doing here?"

"I don't know," he answered grimly before gesturing to her room. "May I? The hallway isn't the most private place for us to talk."

She nodded, tucked her hair back behind her ears and opened the door wider. "Come in."

While his security detail waited in the hall, Hannah turned on the lights and opened her blinds and smoothed the covers of her rumpled bed.

He glanced around the small, Spartan room with the bouquet of violets in a little glass vase next to the bed. "Why are you still here?"

She winced at his sharp tone. "Because I can't afford to leave."

"You should have told me."

"And what would you have done? Laughed in my face? Or thrown me in prison?"

He shrugged. "I was angry. I still am."

She sat cross-legged on the foot of the bed and tilted her chin up at him. "My father has sent me a credit card and my passport by express mail. It should arrive this afternoon. I'll be leaving soon."

"Not if I arrest you."

"Is that why you brought so many of your palace guard? Expecting me to put up quite a fight, aren't you?"

"You don't sound remorseful at all."

"What can I say that I haven't already said? I've

apologized again and again, and I meant every word—"

"So say it again."

A tiny frisson of sensation raced down her back. Something in his voice hinted at danger. Or perhaps it was the expression in his eyes. But suddenly the room felt sexually charged. "I'm sorry."

"That's it? That's your most sincere, heartfelt apology?"

"I gave you my sincere, heartfelt apology two nights ago and you threw it back in my face."

"So? I want to hear it again. I want to feel your sincerity. I want you to prove your sincerity."

"How?"

His hot amber gaze raked her from head to toe. "I'm sure you can think of something."

A shiver raced through her—nerves, anger, as well as anticipation. "You can't kick me out of your palace and then expect me to invite you into my bed."

"Why not?"

"Because I don't want to sleep with you," she retorted fiercely.

"Good, because I can assure you we won't be sleeping."

"It's not going to happen. You were horrible. Mean. Cruel."

"Yes, yes, I was all of the above. So how will you pleasure me?"

"I won't."

"You will." He closed the distance between them, stopping in front of the bed, his thighs inches from her knees. He was standing so close that Hannah's skin prickled and the fine hair at her nape lifted. Unfortunately there was nowhere to run. Not on the third floor with four security guards outside the door.

"And why would I?" she whispered, licking her dry lips.

"Because I remember what you said, the night of the ball. You said you fell hard for me. You fell in love at first sight. Or did you just make that up along with everything else?"

She stared up into his eyes, feeling his tension. He was hanging on to control by a thread, barely mastering his emotions. "No," she whispered. "I did fall for you, right from the beginning. I knew it was wrong to continue to pretend to be Emmeline but I loved being with you…near you… loved everything about you."

"You loved being with me."

She nodded. "More than I've ever enjoyed being with anyone."

He reached down, slipped a hand into her thick

hair, his fingers tangling the long golden strands. "Just as I've never enjoyed anyone as much as I enjoyed being with you."

The husky note in his voice and the heat in his eyes made her pulse leap and her body warm. Her skin tingled and her nerves fizzed and she had to remind herself to breathe.

"So what do we do now?" he asked, allowing the long strands of her hair to slip through his fingers.

"You're not angry with me?"

His hand moved to her neck, and down, caressing the base of her throat to the pulse that beat so erratically there. "I am, but that doesn't seem to change what I feel for you."

She shivered at his touch. Her mouth had gone dry. "And what do you feel for me?"

Emotion burned in his eyes, making the rich amber irises glow. "Love."

Her heart stuttered and stopped. Air bottled in her lungs, she looked up at him in wonder. "You… love…me?"

He dropped his head, his lips brushing hers. "Fool that I am…yes."

She closed her eyes, heart racing. "Not a fool, Zale, because I love you so very, very much."

"Say it again."

She opened her eyes, looked up at him, seeing the hunger and hope in his eyes. "I love you, Zale. I love you more than I've ever loved anyone."

CHAPTER SIXTEEN

ZALE lay in bed with Hannah in his arms, blinds still open so they could watch the sun set. Moments ago the sky had been a spectacular red and orange but the fiery colors were fading, leaving long lavender shadows to stretch across the plaza. The elegant street lamps at the train station were coming on, shining soft yellow pools of light onto the cobbled street.

They'd been in bed for hours. Had made loved for hours. Their lovemaking warm and tender and bittersweet.

Zale had known since birth he'd have to marry a blue blood, a true princess. He'd known since he was fifteen that princess would be Emmeline.

But in the blink of an eye it had all changed.

He wouldn't be marrying Emmeline.

The woman he loved was definitely not royal.

Duty required that he walk away from Hannah. Common sense suggested the same, and yet somehow she felt as essential to his life as Tinny. And he'd never walk away from Tinny.

But who would assume the throne if he chose Hannah? Who knew this country well enough to lead?

There were cousins, of course, but none of them even lived in Raguva anymore, choosing instead to make their home in far flung places like Sydney and Paris, London, San Francisco and Buenos Aires. Places that were urban, sophisticated, exciting.

On the other hand, he hadn't been living in Raguva when his parents died. He'd been in Madrid, but he had returned, and learned what he needed to know to get the job done and he'd served Raguva well.

Others could do what he had done. His oldest cousin, Emmanuel, was first in line, and a compassionate, educated man. He'd be a quick study but his health was poor. So poor in fact that he and his wife hadn't started a family yet due to Emmanuel's weak heart, which meant succession would once again be an issue.

Emmanuel's younger brother, Nicolas, was next in line and Nicolas was charismatic but a notorious spendthrift. Despite a sizable allowance, he was always in debt and looking for a quick bailout from one family member or another.

No, Nicolas was not an option. He'd ruin Raguva within a year or two.

So who then would be Raguva's king should Zale step down? Who would protect Raguva? Who could put Raguva first?

Hannah reached out, placing her hand on his chest. "Stop," she murmured. "There's nothing to do, nothing to decide. We both know how this plays out. I'm leaving in the morning."

"No."

Her hand caressed the smooth plane of muscle. "I don't want to go, but I can't give you heirs, and you need heirs. Not just an heir and a spare, but a whole brood."

"I won't lose you."

"It will be better once I go. Better to make a quick, clean break. We both know the longer I stay the worse it'll be."

"I've lost so much in my life, Hannah. How can I be expected to give you up, too?"

She was silent a long moment. "I don't know," she said at last. "But it's the only real option. You can't forsake your country, and you need to be here for Tinny."

"Tinny can go wherever we go."

"But the palace is the only home Tinny has ever known. You can't take him from his home. Nor can you walk away from your responsibilities here. You are the king. This is your country. This is your destiny."

He cupped her face in his hands, his expression fierce, his amber eyes burning. "*You* are my destiny. I am sure of it. More sure of it than I've ever been of anything."

She kissed him, once and again. "I love you, Zale, but you're wrong. I can't be your destiny, not when Raguva needs you."

"It's so easy for you to go?"

"No! It's not easy, but if you relinquished your throne for me, you'd come to resent me, and I'd always feel guilty."

"There has to be another way."

Hannah curled closer to him, her cheek pressed to his chest so she could listen to the strong, steady beat. The even steady beat soothed her, reassured her. He was a good man and a true king. "But there isn't, darling. Is there?"

So it was decided. She'd be leaving in the morning. Zale would take her to the airport, and put her on his plane for Dallas.

Decision made, Zale called the palace requesting Chef to send dinner over, and they ate in her room, and drank a bottle of red wine and talked for hours about everything but Hannah's departure in the morning.

At midnight they made love again and talked some more, and then somehow it was dawn, and the sun was rising from behind the mountains, turning the sky pale yellow.

Hannah lay in Zale's arms watching the sky gradually lighten.

She felt Zale's hand in her hair, his fingers threading through the long strands. He hadn't spoken in hours but she could feel the emotion inside of him.

"I know I'm not in a position to be asking for favors," she said softly, breaking the silence, "but I'd like to ask for one anyway. Can I see Tinny one more time before I go?"

Zale didn't answer.

"Just a brief visit," she added. "I'll keep it light. Won't get emotional. Won't make a big deal about saying goodbye."

"I don't know, Hannah. Tinny already thinks you're going to be his sister and he won't understand why you're not there anymore."

"But won't he already be confused as to why I'm not there?" She turned in his arms to better see his face. "I can tell Tinny I have to go to Texas to see some of my family, and I'll tell him about Texas and ranches and cowboys." Her eyes searched Zale's. "Please, Zale. It would help me to leave, help me know I haven't just walked away from Tinny as if he didn't matter."

Zale's jaw flexed, his expression taut. "Fine. I'll call Mrs. Sivka and let her know we're taking morning tea with Tinny."

"Thank you."

Three hours later they were sitting down in Tinny's suite at a small table in the living room for morning tea. The table was covered with a cheerful yellow check cloth and a bowl of daisies sat in the middle. Teacups and plates were at each of the three places and Tinny rocked excitedly back and forth in his chair, delighted that he was entertaining.

Mrs. Sivka poured the tea for them, and presented Tinny with his hot chocolate as Hannah entertained Prince Tinny with stories as she'd promised, telling him about Texas and all the animals on their ranch. He liked that they had horses and cows and chickens. He was really excited she'd had a goat.

Hannah loved Tinny's laughter and the way he clapped his hands with excitement. But all too soon teatime was over and they were having to say their goodbyes.

Tinny gave her a big hug and kiss. Hannah

hugged him back. And then she was holding Mrs. Sivka's plump, cool hands in her own.

Mrs. Sivka's blue eyes watered, she squeezed Hannah's hands tightly. "I'm sorry, Your Highness."

Hannah gulped a breath, fighting tears of her own. "Oh, Mrs. Sivka, you can't call me that anymore. I'm just plain Hannah Smith."

"Never plain." Mrs. Sivka's hands squeezed hers. "Take care of yourself."

"I will," Hannah assured her.

"And be happy."

Hannah's smile faltered. "I'll try."

Then Zale's hand was at her elbow and he was ushering her out the door and down the grand staircase to the waiting limousine. The drive to the royal airport was a quiet one and it was even more strained as he escorted her onto his private plane.

Zale could hardly look at Hannah as she sat down in the jet's leather armchair, his handsome features hard, expression savage. "And I'm just supposed to leave you like this?" he demanded, voice harsh.

She'd made up her mind in the limousine she wouldn't cry as they parted, had told herself she'd keep it together for both their sake, and she was determined to keep her vow. "Yes."

His jaw clamped tight. His cheekbones jutted. "And what am I supposed to say now?"

A lump filled her throat, and a terrible tenderness ached in her chest. Her eyes drank him in, trying to remember every feature, every expression. How she loved this man. How she'd miss him.

Her nails dug into her palms. Her eyes were scalding hot. "You say goodbye."

"No."

She would not cry. Not cry. Not, would not. Rising, she caught his handsome face in her hands, looked into his eyes then kissed him gently, tenderly. "Goodbye, Zale. It's time to let me go."

Zale was in hell. A hell unlike any other hell he'd ever known, and he'd known hell before. He'd suffered terribly when Stephen was fighting leukemia. He'd raged when his brother later died. He'd mourned his parents after their plane crashed and cried in private for Tinny who missed his mother every night, not understanding why she wouldn't come home.

But none of that sorrow, none of that loss, was like the pain he felt now because Hannah had given him something no one else had—peace. With Hannah he felt complete. Strong. Whole.

He hadn't realized until she'd arrived in Raguva how empty he'd been, how hollow he'd felt.

Yes, he'd known duty and he'd fulfilled his responsibilities but he'd been like a man sleepwalking. He'd been numb, just going through the motions. And then she arrived and brought him to life.

And now she was gone. His woman. And she'd taken his heart.

For two endless weeks Zale barely spoke, moving silently from bedchamber to office, to parapet and back again.

He ate little. Slept less. He wouldn't even allow Krek to attend to him. When he wasn't working he ran. He ran early in the morning, in the middle of the day and late into the night. And when he couldn't run anymore, he stretched out on his bed and prayed.

He prayed as he hadn't prayed in years. Not since Stephen was ill and Zale wanted him cured.

Zale's prayers hadn't been heard then but he prayed anyway now.

He loved her. He needed her. Fiery, passionate, fierce, funny Hannah.

She was flawed and stubborn, impetuous and emotional and he'd never loved anyone more.

His eyes stung and he rubbed at them. He hadn't

cried since he'd had to comfort Tinny after their parents funeral, and he wouldn't cry now, but his heart was breaking and there was nothing he could do about it. Life was life and it'd dealt him a bitter hand.

It had been nearly a month since Hannah had gone and Zale had run himself to the point of exhaustion. But the exhaustion failed to dull the pain. His heart hurt—burned—constantly and he couldn't understand how that part of him could hurt so much when the rest of him felt dead.

He was standing at his window in his study, staring out at nothing when a knock sounded on his door.

The door opened and Mrs. Sivka entered looking so much frailer than she had a month ago. It was as if she'd aged ten years in thirty days. "Forgive me for intruding, Your Majesty, but I insisted that your staff let me in to see you."

Zale had been pacing his office, unable to sit, unable to rest and he walked away from her, to the window overlooking the garden. He kept his back to her so she couldn't see his face. "Is Tinny not well?"

"The prince is fine. He's with Mrs. Daum right now. But I need a word with you."

"What is it?"

She was silent so long that he glanced over his shoulder. "Mrs. Sivka?" he prompted impatiently.

Anxiety was etched into her features and worry in her eyes. "There is something I've never told anyone. Something I swore I would never tell. It was a blood oath. One of those promises you cannot break, for any reason, ever. And I haven't."

Zale sighed, irritated. He was tired, not in the mood for this. The past month had been absolute hell and the last thing he wanted was to play word games. "And yet you feel the need to break it now?" he drawled sarcastically.

"Yes."

He turned around, folded his arms across his chest. "Why?"

"It might change everything."

No, he really couldn't deal with her now, not if she insisted on talking about secrets and blood vows and other silly games. "What would?"

"The truth."

"Mrs. Sivka, *please.*"

Her round face creased. "There were two babies, Your Majesty. Two baby girls, not one. Princess Emmeline and the infant princess, Jacqueline."

Zale blinked. He'd heard what she said but it hadn't fully registered. "What?"

"Princess Emmeline was one of two. She had a twin sister."

"That's nonsense. Absolute fiction. King William would have told me if Emmeline had a twin—"

"He didn't know. No one knew—"

"Listen to yourself, Mrs. Sivka! I'm not Tinny. Not interested in make-believe."

"This is true. I was there. I was there for Princess Jacqueline's delivery at Marmont, the royal family's hunting lodge in northern Brabant. Her Royal Highness's nanny had been my best friend since childhood, and she'd asked me to be there, too, at the delivery. I was to take care of the newborn for the first few days while she tended to Princess Jacqueline."

Mrs. Sivka took a quick breath, expression pleading, wanting him to understand, needing him to understand. "Of course I went, and we thought we were prepared for the delivery. It was a difficult delivery. No one expected twins, and although there was a midwife on hand, it became apparent that something was very wrong. Her Highness needed surgery. She was bleeding internally. But as you know, Marmont is remote, at least an hour's drive from the nearest city, much less a modern hospital. We called for help but there was no helicopter available, no emergency medical team near us."

Her eyes turned pink and her mouth pressed thin. "Her Highness knew she was dying—"

She broke off as tears fell and she struggled to keep control. "Her Royal Highness was very brave, and quite calm. She was also very specific about what she wanted us to do. One baby was to go to her brother at the palace in Brabant. And the other baby was to go to the babies' father in America. I took infant Princess Jacqueline to him with the news that Her Royal Highness had died in childbirth but she wanted him to have their child—"

"He knew Jacqueline had been pregnant?"

Mrs. Sivka nodded. "Her Royal Highness had written to him, told him, but her family wouldn't give him access to her."

"I can't believe this."

Mrs. Sivka's shoulders twisted. "But I never told him he had another daughter. I couldn't, not after the vow I made."

Zale was absolutely numb. "Why tell me this now?"

"Because it changes everything."

"It changes nothing."

"You're not listening then."

"I am listening. Fairy tales and secrets and blood vows—"

"You don't have to be afraid, Your Majesty."

"Afraid?" he roared, hands clenched, fury blinding him. "You think I'm afraid?"

"Yes." She folded her arms across her middle. "You did this very same thing when you were just a boy. You hated to be disappointed, hated pain, so you'd hurt yourself first so no one could make you hurt worse."

"You can go, Mrs. Sivka."

Mrs. Sivka didn't budge. "Your Majesty, prayers do get answered, and there is goodness and justice in the world, not just pain. Because in your heart you already know the ending of my story."

Zale ground his teeth together, muscles so tense he ached all over. "That what? This infant princess...this Jacqueline...?"

"Is your Princess Hannah."

Zale sat down abruptly on the windowsill, his legs no longer able to hold him.

Can't be.

Can't.

Impossible.

"You shouldn't tell tales," he said roughly, hating Mrs. Sivka in that moment for torturing him like this when he had nothing left to go on. He needed to eat, needed to sleep, but most of all, he needed her, Hannah, his woman.

"I've never lied to you, Your Majesty. I wouldn't

start now." Mrs. Sivka went to the door, opened it, revealing a wan-looking Hannah dressed in jeans and a white blouse, her hair loose and her stunning face scrubbed free of all makeup.

Hannah looked at him from across the library, blue eyes huge in her pale face. "Hello, Your Majesty."

Zale couldn't breathe. Hannah. Here.

Here.

And his. Princess or not. It didn't matter. It would never matter. He'd gladly give up everything for a chance at a life with her.

Mrs. Sivka smiled broadly. "Your Majesty, may I present to you, Her Royal Highness, Hannah Jacqueline Smith."

Zale didn't know who moved first—he or Hannah—but suddenly she was in his arms in the middle of the study, her arms wrapped tightly around his neck.

"I never thought I'd see you again," she choked out, voice wobbling as she looked up into his face. "And never is such a long, long time."

"I know. I've been so angry this past month. I was going mad without you here."

"I heard."

"How?"

"I called the palace every day and talked to Mrs.

Sivka or Krek, asking about you. It killed me to hear that you were so unhappy."

He clasped her face in his hands. "My staff talked about me behind my back?"

"Yes. Sorry. But I badgered them until they told me the truth. I had to know." Her eyes filled with tears. "And I'd lose it, absolutely lose it when I heard you were running fifteen, twenty miles a day and not eating. I wanted to jump on a plane and come see you but I was afraid that if I came, I'd never leave."

"But you're here now."

She blinked, and tears fell in streaks. "Because I don't ever intend to leave. Not unless you forcibly throw me onto the streets."

Her blue eyes had turned aquamarine from crying and her long black lashes were wet and matted and her nose was pink and she was the most beautiful woman he'd ever seen. "I need you here, Hannah. I can't do this without you. I don't even want to live without you."

"That's what Mrs. Sivka said when I called her on Tuesday. She said she feared for you, feared you'd become too self-destructive, and that's when she told me who I was." She bit into her lip to stop it quivering. "The name on my birth certificate is Hannah Jacqueline Smith. I always wondered where my father got the name Jacqueline. He never told me, not until this week after Mrs. Sivka told me everything."

Zale turned to look at Mrs. Sivka. "I can't believe you waited this long to tell her the truth! You could have cleared this all up weeks ago—"

"I'd made a promise, Your Majesty."

"Ridiculous," he muttered, adding something under his breath about old women and blood vows before clasping Hannah's face in his hands and kissing her brow, her damp cheek, her salty lips.

Hannah laughed against his mouth. "Don't be mean," she whispered. "At least she told us."

"I should fire her. Throw her out—"

"Zale!" Hannah drew back and gave him a stern look. "She's your nanny!"

Zale gazed down into her eyes, his expression hard and then turning to awe. "And she knew you before I did. She was there at your birth. Incredible." And it was incredible, he thought, drinking her in. Hannah wasn't ordinary Hannah Smith, but Emmeline's twin sister, and a true princess of Brabant. "It's a miracle."

"It is," she agreed. "And my father supports Mrs. Sivka's story. She did bring me to him when I was just a week old."

"He must be stunned to discover he has another daughter."

Hannah hesitated. "I haven't told him that part yet. I thought I would, when he flies in for our wedding."

The corner of Zale's mouth slowly curved. "And when is our wedding, Your Highness?"

Hannah grinned back. "Mrs. Sivka and I were thinking maybe a week from today?"

Zale glanced at his beaming nanny. "You're planning my wedding now, are you, Mrs. Sivka?"

"Why not? I used to change your nappies."

"You may go, Mrs. Sivka," Zale said with mock sternness.

"Yes, Your Majesty," she answered, heading for the door. But Zale called to her before she could close the door. "Mrs. Sivka?"

His nanny looked at him with terrible tenderness. "Yes, Your Majesty?"

"Thank you." His eyes were warm, his expression grateful. "Thank you for everything."

"My pleasure."

Once she was gone, Zale lifted Hannah onto the corner of her desk and moved between her legs to get as close to her as he could. "What kind of wedding do you want, Hannah?"

"I don't care, as long as you and I are both there."

She reached for his hips, pulled him even closer, so that his zipper rubbed up against her inner thighs. "People are going to talk, though," she added, sliding a hand over his crotch and his growing erection. "How will you explain that I'm not Princess Emmeline, but Hannah?"

"Princess Hannah," he corrected, trying not to be distracted by the heat of her hand on his aching shaft. "Emmeline's twin sister, and a Princess of Brabant." He lowered his head, brushed his lips across hers and then kissed her again, wetting her lips with a flick of his tongue. "My Princess of Brabant."

She gasped and shivered against him, her hands pressed to his chest. "Um, King Patek, can we lock the door?"

"I think that's an excellent idea." He cupped her face, kissed her deeply, parting her lips to take her mouth completely. "Can't wait to do that to your body," he growled. "I've missed you. Missed everything about you."

She kissed him back, legs wrapping around his hips, so turned on she was trembling. "Zale, I love you."

"Not as much as I love you."

The corner of her mouth tilted in a wicked little

smile as she lightly scratched her nails down his chest. "Prove it."

"Don't you worry, Princess. I will."

EPILOGUE

IT WAS late. It had been a long day, and Zale was only now heading for Tinny's rooms to say good-night to his brother.

But reaching Tinny's living room, Zale's tension and exhaustion eased, his shoulders relaxing as he spotted Hannah already there, sitting on the couch with Tinny reading him his favorite bedtime story.

Zale stood in the doorway a moment, content to just look at them and listen.

Hannah, his beloved princess, pregnant with his first child. And sweet, innocent Tinny who absolutely adored Hannah with all his heart.

What could be better? What more could a man want?

What more could a king need?

And for a moment his chest squeezed so tight Zale couldn't breathe.

To think that the randomness of life could take Stephen and his parents, but save Tinny, and then give him Hannah?

To think that an impostor princess could turn out to be the real thing?

Impossible that Hannah was Princess Jacqueline's other daughter, Emmeline's missing twin and the keeper of his heart.

Zale felt hot emotion sweep through him, constricting his chest.

If Hannah and Emmeline hadn't met in Palm Beach...

If Emmeline hadn't asked Hannah to switch places...

If Hannah hadn't come to Raguva...

If Mrs. Sivka hadn't broken her vow...

He gave his head a faint shake, overwhelmed all over again by fate. So many things could have gone wrong. So many things could have kept him from Hannah...

But they hadn't.

Suddenly Hannah looked up, brow furrowed and then seeing him, she smiled. "You're just in time for the last chapter."

Her smile made him ache and it was almost too much, almost too strong, this fierce love he felt for her.

"Good," he said, moving into the room and sitting down on the couch next to Hannah and Tinny. "This is my favorite part."

"Because you love happy endings," she said, smiling at him, her love for him so transparent, warming her beautiful blue eyes and curving her generous mouth.

"I do," he answered, taking her hand and carrying it to his mouth. "Are you tired? Is the baby kicking too much?"

She touched her round belly. "He was, but now I think he's listening. He knows his daddy is here."

"Shall I read the last chapter then? Would you like that, Tinny?" Zale offered.

"Yes, Zale," Tinny said, taking the book from Hannah's hands and pressing it into his brother's. "Yes, read it. Read it right now."

Hannah laughed softly as the baby inside her kicked hard just then, a vigorous one-two. "I think your future footballer agrees," she said, running her fingers across her ribs where the kick had been.

Zale's eyes gleamed. "He does have a good kick, doesn't he?"

"Most definitely." She leaned back, resting her head on his shoulder. "Now read, please. I'm anxious to get to the part where the prince marries the princess and they all live happily ever after."

"And they did, didn't they?" he said, opening to the first page of the last chapter.

Her voice grew husky. "Yes. Yes, Your Majesty, they did. Very happily."

* * * * *